The Chant of Jimmie Blacksmith

THOMAS KENEALLY

Published by Angus and Robertson · Publishers

The Chant of Jimmie Blacksmith

Also by Thomas Keneally

THE PLACE AT WHITTON

THE FEAR

BRING LARKS AND HEROES

THREE CHEERS FOR THE PARACLETE

THE SURVIVOR

A DUTIFUL DAUGHTER

ANGUS & ROBERTSON · PUBLISHERS

102 Glover Street, Cremorne, Sydney

2 Fisher Street, London

159 Boon Keng Road, Singapore

P.O. Box 1072, Makati MCC, Rizal, Philippines

West Melbourne

first published in 1972 by

ANGUS AND ROBERTSON (PUBLISHERS) PTY LTD

Reprinted 1972, 1975

National Library of Australia
card number and ISBN 0 207 12375 6

Registered in Australia for transmission by post as a book

PRINTED IN GREAT BRITAIN

To the memory of

PETER CADY

✝ *January, 1971*

1

IN JUNE of 1900 Jimmie Blacksmith's maternal uncle Tabidgi—Jackie Smolders to the white world—was disturbed to get news that Jimmie had married a white girl in the Methodist church at Wallah.

Therefore he set out with Jimmie's initiation tooth to walk a hundred miles to Wallah. The tooth would be a remonstration and lay a tribal claim on Jimmie. For Tabidgi Jackie Smolders was full-blooded and of the Tullam section of the Mungindi tribe. To his mind people should continue to wed according to the tribal pattern.

Which was: that Tullam should marry Mungara, Mungara should wed Garri, Garri should wed Wibbera, Wibbera take Tullam's women. But here was Jimmie, a Tullam, married in church to a white girl.

Jackie felt distressed, a spiritual unease over Jimmie Blacksmith's wedding. These tribal arrangements should still be made, Tabidgi Jackie Smolders thought. The elders kept the tribal pattern in their heads and could arrange a tribal wedding even if the Tullam buck was on a mission station eighty miles, two hundred miles, from Mungara woman.

Jackie Smolders was therefore dispirited—so too even his flippant sister, a full-blooded lady called Dulcie Blacksmith. Half-breed Jimmie had resulted from a visit some white man had made to Brentwood blacks' camp in 1878. The mission-

1

aries—who had never been told the higher things of Wibbera —had made it clear that if you had pale children it was because you'd been rolled by white men. They had not been told that it was Emu-Wren, the tribal totem, who quickened the womb.

Mrs Dulcie Blacksmith believed the missionaries more or less. They took such a low view of lying in other people that they were unlikely to lie themselves. And certainly, Mrs Blacksmith had been rolled by white men. For warmth in winter, she once said. For warmth in winter and for comfort in summer. But the deep truth was that Emu-Wren had quickened Jimmie Blacksmith (pale or not) in the womb and that Mungara owed him a woman.

Yet here he was marrying a white girl off a farm.

Therefore off went Jackie Smolders carrying Jimmie's initiation tooth wrapped in clean flour-cloth and carried in the left pocket, away from the sevenpence that belonged to the right pocket and might be infected with malchance.

It must be said that although Jackie Smolders was alcoholic and knew that Jimmie Blacksmith was earning wages which Jackie, as maternal uncle, could claim for liquor, his chief reason for setting out towards Wallah was tribal and centred in the magical tooth.

The tooth had been knocked out of Jimmie's mouth by Mungindi elders when the boy was thirteen, in 1891. So too he had been circumcised with stone, the incision poulticed over with chalk-clay and likewise the eyes. It is necessary to take cognizance of Jimmy Blacksmith's experience from the day of this initiation to the time in 1900 that Jackie Smolders went to Wallah.

When Jimmie was taken from camp for his initiation, Dulcie Blacksmith presumed him dead for the time being. The epoch-old agenda of ceremonies was kept a secret from all the women. As far as Dulcie knew, the great Lizard had mashed and swallowed him and would now give birth to him as a completed Mungindi man.

He was gone for weeks. The mission station superintendent, Rev. H. J. Neville, B.A., kept asking where Jimmie was but was not incommoded with any part of the truth.

Grown Mungindi men—Jackie Smolders for example—knew

2

that Jimmie was hiding in the scrub close to an anabranch of
the Macquarie River. Here he waited for the wound to heal
and lived on possum meat. He was full of the exhilaration of
tribal manhood and the relief of finding that the lizard story
was not true to the extent of his being actually chewed or
swallowed. He sang:

Dash surprise from your eyes, my mother,
As crested parrots are dashed from the white branches of
dawn.
On your brow put pride as proud as Dubra the berry tree.
Out of the chrysalis and out of the lizard's mouth your son
comes man.

Sometimes he swung the bull-roarer lest any woman from
Brentwood mission come near. If seen by a woman during
your isolation, you were hexed beyond knowing. Women in
their turn were raised to fear the voice of the bull-roarer. If
you twirled it now and again, you were more or less safe.

Jimmie Blacksmith's initiation took place in autumn. There
had been very little rain, and no frosts yet. The winds shifted,
casual and warm, under a high Easter sun.

Back at Brentwood, the Rev. H. J. Neville could have used
a good boy like Jimmie for the Easter hymns.

"Blasted blacks!" he told his wife. "The best of them are
likely to vanish at any time."

He felt that Jimmie was a protégé and had a sobriety none
of his half-siblings possessed. The European who had im-
pregnated giddy Dulcie Blacksmith must have been of a pensive nature; a man who perhaps hated the vice of sleeping with
black women yet could not master it. Mr Neville himself had
often felt the distinctive pull of some slant-grinned black face.

Townspeople spoke of this sin as if it were a distinctive
form of immorality, substantially different from fornicating
with a white woman. It was an accredited old wives' tale that
by lying with blacks a white man was gradually reduced to
impotence with white women.

Good Mr Neville now reached for the butter at table and
found the flies about it as thick almost as at high summer.

"If a person could be certain," he said, a little peevishly, "that he had imbued *one* of them with decent ambitions!"

Until Jimmie Blacksmith vanished, Mr Neville had thought that he had a chance of bringing off the trick with eager, sober, polite Jimmie Blacksmith.

The Rev. Mr Neville had a true evangelical vocation. If he had been a student of anthropology he would have been less baffled before his fly-blown butter dish at Easter, 1891. Anthropology was a word he had never heard. It was, as well, a two-way traffic, demanding a specialized white awareness and talkative natives. Jimmie felt it would have been bad-mannered to upset Mr Neville by being talkative about initiation.

Since the boy's disappearance, Mr Neville had taken to cutting even more notifications of vacant ministries out of the *Methodist Church Times*. All over the little weatherboard manse were mislaid small squares of newsprint proposing pastorages, anchorages, from the Riverina to the Darling Downs. They yellowed in the high autumn sun, in Jimmie Blacksmith's lasting absence; while H. J. Neville continued faithful to his dull wife amidst such cheap, such wantonly appealing black flesh.

For some days Jimmie's incised genitals stung beyond bearing. He would sing:

In the sting of our manhood,
Mungara's daughters being few
As hills beyond Marooka, river snake—scant hills,
Mungara's daughters scant,
Over Marooka we went singing,
Stalking Widgarra under dusty suns,
Came roaring at them from the moon
Painting blood on Widgarra men with strokes of warclubs,
Taking to us all the shrilling pee-wit women,
daughters to Mungara,
Wives unto the men of Emu-Wren.

He sang it in monotone and with dissonances Mr Neville would have found strange. It was a fine song about an ancient raid. The woman-stealing it recounted had taken place during the English civil war, two and a half centuries previously.

4

Apart from the itch, he had all the comforts. A blanket. His mission clothes. Fresh-water crayfish and slightly muddy perch, left land-locked when the river took a new course, were plentiful. Possums came out at night. He flung his club at their phosphorescent eyes.

Ten days after Easter, Jimmie reappeared at Brentwood.

His half-sister, Bibra Dottie Blacksmith, was the first to notice his quiet entry. Then some other women and his half-brother Morton.

Dottie ran before him ululating in her high fifteen-year-old voice:

"Born from the Lizard comes my shining brother Tullam man."

Morton woke Jimmie's presumptive father, Wilf Blacksmith, who was well on the way to death, only a few years away, by pneumonia and alcohol. Dulcie dropped a shirt of Wilf's that she had been washing in a basin in the sun. She shivered, for—with Jimmie's manhood accomplished—the cold weather had already set in.

Dulcie could see her son coming through the loose thicket where the hovels of Brentwood stood. The sun emphasized his funny pale hair. Men hooted his passage in a comradely way. Small children ran across his path. Piercing the day, Bibra Dottie's voice sang the news:

"Out of the monster's mouth, sealed in manhood, comes my Tullam brother."

How Dulcie laughed! She and Morton laughed wildly on solemn occasions and Mr Neville therefore thought them dense. It was not the truth.

"Where yer bin, yer paley bastard?" Dulcie screamed in the crisp, Cockneyfied version of English that natives spoke. Still holding Wilf's irrelevant stained shirt she picked up the song from Dottie.

"Out of the Lizard's belly come my sons, crushing frost, making large marks on the earth, sons returning in manhood who were sucklings from my belly, born to Emu-Wren by me."

Mr Neville had watched from his veranda the return of young Jimmie Blacksmith.

"Excitable people," he murmured. "Excitable people."

It made him happy to see them. God must love those who greet mere absentees with so much ardour. It was as if the boy had come back from the dead.

Mr Neville wondered if, this once, he might get a sensible, explicit answer from a black. He walked down the path and out onto the dusty grass of the mission station.

"Jimmie Blacksmith!" he called. His voice cut the shrilling off. When Jimmie broke off his path and came towards the missioner, his brother Morton staggered about with the hilarity of it. But there was silence. Jimmie's feet could be heard padding the earth in their light economic way.

"Where have you been, Master Blacksmith?"

"Catchin' possums."

Mr Neville flinched. "I can't understand you. Didn't it occur to you you might be needed for higher things? The Easter choir perhaps?"

"How d'yer mean, Mr Neville?"

"You've missed a lot of school."

"Yair, Mr Neville."

"Very well. You must come to my study, please."

In the study, a front sitting-room dignified by desk, an *orbis terrarum*, three shelves of standard evangelical works, Jimmie was caned for truancy. No one resented it. No one had hindered Mungindi elders from gathering to make Jimmie a man. Though they had come from places spread over more than two thousand squares miles to initiate him, it would have seemed no unworthy usage that their new buck should now be lashed on the arse by a Methodist minister. For the truth of Mr Neville and the truth of Emu-Wren ran parallel. Mr Neville had his place, as did the poor-bugger-white-fella-son-of-God-got-nailed.

"Cane teach yer to be good feller now," Wilf stated. "Don' let that stand in yer light."

2

JIMMIE, who had come home from his initiation suffused with tribal manhood, began—during the next three years, by his own insight and under the Nevilles' influence—to question its value.

What did Tullam and Mungara stand for now? Tribal men were beggars puking Hunter River rotgut sherry in the lee of hotel shit-houses. Tribal elders, who cared for initiation teeth and knew where the soul-stones of each man were hidden and how the stones could be distinguished, lent out their wives to white men for a suck from a brandy bottle.

Mr and Mrs Neville spoke to Jimmie of other matters than tribal.

"If you could ever find a nice girl off a farm to marry, your children would only be quarter-caste then, and your grandchildren one-eighth caste, scarcely black at all."

Most men who weren't old men had become a little sceptical of the tribal cosmogony, even if they were not as clear-headed about it as Jimmie. The very height of tribal manhood for some was this gulping of cheap wine in pub yards. That activity itself was a tortured questing after a new world picture for Mungindi man.

The country police did not take that view of the matter.

In the spring of 1894 the Rev. Mr Neville was awarded the

Methodist church in Muswellbrook, and asked if Jimmie could come with him as some sort of servant or houseboy.

"Yer gotter better yerself, Jimmie," said Dulcie.

A dray jolted the Nevilles and Jimmie away towards the railhead, Mr Neville waving a great deal, even if soberly. He felt some guilt at giving up Brentwood for some easy white church and seemed to be trying to impress his concern upon the Brentwood air, plastically, with his hand.

Dulcie sang:

> *Tall is my son going away.*
> *The mountains will feel his heel,*
> *And his hair catch in the stars.*

She would scarcely ever see him again.

The train crossed mountains he had not seen before, and came down to Muswellbrook, a green town on river flats. There was a broad still river, and weatherboard and stone houses from the curve of the high street all the way down to the banks.

In a landscape of such promise, Jimmie thought again of Mrs Neville's words: "If you could ever find a nice girl off a farm . . ."

He had very nearly decided that it would be better to have children who were scarcely black at all.

Mrs Neville taught him to cook, even chicken with seasoning. Mr Neville spoke to him of the size of the earth.

"And where are we on the globe, Jimmie?"

"We're here, Mister Neville."

His index finger would jab at a point on the *orbis terrarum*, understanding that that finger could not be pointed sharply enough to indicate the small places where Tullam and Mungara were prescriptive. Not that Jimmie assumed anything was right or wrong merely by size. Still, the large earth did indeed swamp them.

Jimmie's black soul had been most undermined by the train journey, by seeing the umber plains which he had thought to be the total universe lead the Nevilles and himself to heights where red cedars stood so tall that the mind and the sky were stretched, through sub-tropic passes where the giant fern seeped a clear and (one felt) purified water, much more crystalline than the racy and unracing waters of the shallow Macquarie.

The strangler vines were flowering in their hold on the lean trunks of mountain ash.

"That there, Jimmie," Mr Neville had said, "is a manna tree. It has a hard sweet gum that can be eaten. I believe the black people on this side of the mountains set great store by it."

Earlier in the year, before the Nevilles and Jimmie came, the valley had flooded, enriching the top soil of the lower flats to a pitch of improbable green. The sweet pastures and vineyards resounded in Jimmie Blacksmith's nervous system, conveying the fact of tidy white ownership, dislodging Tullam and Mungara.

Out on visitation, Jimmie used to drive Mr and Mrs Neville in their light new dray. Mr Neville's conversation was often instructive.

"That tree there is the *Eucalyptus gigans*. It has been introduced to the isle of Cyprus, I believe, with resounding results."

Oxalis ran yellow up and down the aisles of the orchards.

"The gold is welcome," said Mr Neville. "But there, that purple on the embankment, that is far from welcome. It is Mediterranean bugloss. The Hunter River people call it Patterson's Curse."

Or again, "They have begun an open-cut coal mine down the valley. A fine outcrop of coal, a godsend. They call it Greta. You don't have to go down into the mine, you see, you don't have to ruin your lungs. You work on the surface. You dig into the hillside. It might be possible one day for you to get work there, Jimmie."

Mr Neville was happy now, in a decent pastorate in a decent town. He knew that the white women with their corseted bounteous wombs would not tempt as he had been tempted at Brentwood.

Going to the butcher's for Mrs Neville, Jimmie Blacksmith saw a kinsman squatted in the shade of a draper's shop. It was a man called Wongee Tom Carstairs, aged about forty.

Wongee Tom demonstrated Wilf Blacksmith's dictum:

9

Black feller kin eat,
Black feller kin drink.
Black feller can't do both
And drinkin's happier.

Wongee Tom was sleeping off his happiness but had one eye out for friends, such as Jimmie. His cheeks folded themselves strangely into creases of apparent contentment.

"Hey, yer paley bastard!" he murmured.

"Hey, Wongee Tom."

"Yair, that's who. How's that old sow Dulcie goin'?"

"Dulcie's good. Wilf's drunk." It was a safe enough prediction. "Dottie's good, Mort's bloody good. Are you good?"

"Yair, not workin' much." He chuckled at his own joke. They could get very superior, these travelled blacks who had seen the large towns.

"Are there other Emu-Wren here?" Jimmie asked in Mungindi.

"Emu-Wren?" Wongee Tom mocked. "Bullshit." But he gave in to the old language. "I've come a big walk from Brentwood, walking all the way. Hardly a black man to offer me a roll of his wife. No Emu-Wren. I don't know why I left the plains. The crayfish here are good. Nice red meat."

"You got a job?" Jimmie asked. In English, for in Mungindi there was no word for *job*.

"I catch 'em possums. Sell 'em skin. Thrippence a skin. Not much. Wish I had a gun. Whitefeller don't like Wongee hangin' round homestead catchin' possums. *You bugger off, blackie!* Thrippence a skin, that's all."

"Long time since yer skinned yer last possum," Jimmie Blacksmith teased him.

"Like hell, yer paley bastard!" Then Wongee Tom gave in and laughed out his admissions. "Don' know when last one was. Possum meat scrawny, full of bones. Wongee rather pinch bacon."

Both black men sat, watching a farmer's family, who had crossed the pavement to the draper's door.

From within came the gurgle of the store-owner welcoming custom. The mother and three girls passed both black men without a glance. All of these were sucking with a vary-

10

ing degree of blatancy and a half-pound bag of boiled sweets was secure in the possession of the eldest girl. Only the youngest, perhaps four, blue-eyed beneath a sailor's cap on which was printed *H.M.S. Sugar and Spice*, delayed at the door to look full at Wongee Tom. Already, it seemed, she knew that she must take whatever chances of direct gazing came to her, since her mother would soon have her taught to observe such people only obliquely, in a manner that did little for one's knowledge.

Wongee smiled at her tolerantly. "Yer oughter come back twenty years' time, plant them blue eyes on Wongee. . . ."

The little girl ducked away from the proposal and into the draper's gloom, where her mother was testing the strength of a square of serge.

"Oughtn't say that sort of thing, Wongee. Give us a bad name."

H.M.S. Sugar and Spice dashed past them as her family left the store, the tough square mother bound flinty-eyed for her next shopping task.

"Would you like a white woman, Wongee?" Jimmie Black-smith asked Wongee—since Mrs Neville had mentioned the possibility for him.

"Don't seem ter make the cow-cockies happy, having white woman for 'is wife. Why else he come after black girls? Must be sum'pin to white women we ain't been told."

They went on sitting and spoke of other things. When Jimmie next saw the family of girls, the eldest was carrying a new spirit heater; and her mother, all at once, authorized all the younger ones to partake of the confectioner's viaticum the big sister carried half open beside the heater.

Jimmie Blacksmith fell in love with the eldest girl without delay. He wanted her homesomeness, the density of her air of family security; the way she carried and gave away, unself-consciously bountiful, the barley-sugar, the family eucharist.

And with love, ambitions! The sort Mrs Neville wanted him to have, landowning ambitions, ambitions for contracts, for bonding one's word and sticking to a job until it was finished.

The girl went by in sturdy clothes and a light film of brown dust on her strenuously buffed boots. He watched her

11

full-fleshed waist recede, and never saw her again.

"Ay," said Wongee Tom, "yer wouldn't mind that fat girl! Yer stalky bastard!"

If he had looked upon his black initiation in an evangelical way, he might have come to call this moment the one in which he lost his black core. It had been eroded by the Nevilles' ceaseless European pride—the acclaim of gum-trees in far places, the schooling in the globe and the bulk of things British, let alone European. Even by the bright oxalis in the orchards, or talk of the open-cut at Greta.

"I think I might git a job in the open-cut," he said suddenly.

"Diggin' coal?"

"Yair. I'll git a job there."

"There's a woman here," Wongee Tom said in the tribal language. "She isn't Mungara. She yawns for men and not with her mouth. She weeps for men and not with her eyes. She drinks men down, she is a cave for men." He laughed. In English he said: "But she don't keep the rain off. We git together in the paddock behind the Caledonian. We git a young whitefeller buy us sherry. We gotter drink 'im bloody fast because bloody p'lice come round every hour. But there's lubras round all the time, but this special one, Lucy, see."

Suddenly he sounded urgent. "Don' git a job in the open-cut. Come round to the Caledonian Sat'dee night. Is all a poor black bastard got left."

The Saturday night was a visit to hell. All creeping through fences, tripping on tussocks, passing money to white boys who, on the whole, were honest and brought back sherry.

The remote laughter of whites in the Caledonian, then the sizzle of liquor down his throat, the bursting radiance of it in his chest. "Too much!" he tried to say. But it was warm.

Time moved in jerks. Suddenly he was retching; suddenly pouring himself without joy into one of the women.

Hiding in the long grass when the police made their rounds. Someone belching. Someone tittering at someone belching.

More fire in his throat. Dark hands forcing bottles and thighs on him.

12

As well as jerking forward, time made events seem almost simultaneous to drunk Jimmie Blacksmith, made of hours one reeling, rutting, reeking moment.

He was arrested but didn't know it.

He woke, shivering and indoors, and the first voice he heard was Mr Neville's.

". . . always been exemplary."

"Never wandered orf?" .

"Once when he was a child. Some years ago now. At Brentwood."

"They think it's their right to wander orf."

"Not Jimmie. He works well. Sticks to a job."

Suddenly Jimmie, who had awoken with a sense of isolation, understood and looked where he was. Someone had, it seemed, put him down on a bunk with accuracy and then he had fallen into the tangle of aboriginal legs, heads and pudenda on the floor. There was, of course, a stink of old vomit.

A constable whose trousers were dangerously long for such sticky treading came along the corridor to the cells.

"Right! Jimmie Blacksmith?"

"Me, boss."

"Yore friggin' luck! A reverind's come for yer. And Mrs Reverind too. Hope yer know how to behave fuckin' grateful."

"Yair."

"Orright." He unlocked the cell door. No one on the floor moved. They lay like figures in a massacre. "Don't tread on no one's balls. Git orf to the pump and wash yerself down."

It was very early, cock-crow in the yard, and an icicle hung from the pump. Jimmie washed himself unsparingly in front of the constable. He felt elated, enough to pity the policeman. Jimmie Blacksmith was baptizing himself a white man, whereas there was nothing the constable could baptize himself. He was doomed to a broken-pillar monument in Muswellbrook graveyard, with *Raised by Subscription from his Comrades* chiselled on it.

"Christ," the man said, "why've yer gotter be the cleanest fuckin' darkie in Australia? It's cold."

"Won't be a second, boss."

13

But he had taken his shirt off and was bringing freezing handfuls of water to his armpits. Belching secretively, he watched the new sun cut a hard line of shadow across the frost in the yard, encouraging him to be severe with himself, and long-suffering. Property was the key, he understood, and not to give it away to your kin; not when they had thirsts like Wilf or Wongee Tom.

Jimmie Blacksmith told the Nevilles he wanted to leave and get work at the open-cut. They consented, but first they felt they must ascertain—as religious people always need to—that his motives were correct.

"If you get in with that drunken crowd you won't be given a job, and if you are, you won't keep it."

"That mob make me feel sick, Mr Neville. I don't want that crowd. I gotter start working so I kin git property."

"I'll give you a reference," Mr Neville said, and looked for a second, without seeming much comforted, into his wife's approving face.

They did not want even to look at Mr Neville's reference when he tried there for work.

But Jimmie would not descend to muttered black curses.

"Orright, boss," he said; and tried to find work in the orchards. But there had been an economic depression, they told him, and itinerant whites had taken all the work there was.

At last he was lucky enough to get a contract from an Irish farmer up river. One of those harsh, commercially-minded Irishmen with a fat, bleak-eyed young wife to sit by his fire and ponder on the crucifix above it.

Middle-aged farmers with prescriptive plump wife and crucifix are not known to be generous. The basis of the contract was this. One of Healy's pastures ran uphill into forest, and cows had therefore been occasionally lost and stolen. Jimmie was to make a forest fence, post-and-rail hardwood, posts seven feet apart, going rate one shilling and sixpence a rod, to be finished by the end of September. It would cost Healy £2 12s. 2d.

The Irishman was always delivering ultimatums and stepping up close to Jimmie. He had a large square beard like a nobleman called the Duke of Clarence, whom Mr Neville had

14

once shown Jimmie a photograph of and, in a spasm of reck-
lessness, even whispered that there were people who thought
the duke was Jack the Ripper. Like the duke, Healy had the
air of a basilisk.

"Yer have any religion? Other than nigger?"

"Methodist, boss."

"Then I give yer me Christian promise that I'll cut yore
bloody black balls out if yer mess this job. And every post
that's out of place an inch, I'll dock yer a shillin'."

"Fair enough, boss." It would be part of his cunning, he
swore, to accept insult as a business proposition.

The means Jimmie used to acquire fencing tools are of
little interest, except that he had stolen the shovel from Mr
Neville's place, knowing where it was kept and not having to
fumble for it in the dark.

Jimmie suspected that there was some sort of justice involved in that theft. Perhaps there was, for the Nevilles were
the ones who, although poor themselves, had taught him that
possession is a sacred state. They had even given him a parting endowment, a small amount; a deposit, they might have
considered it.

Possession was a holy state and he had embarked on it with
the Nevilles' shovel. The Nevilles had succeeded so well as
to make Jimmie a snob. In the mind of the true snob there
are certain limited criteria to denote the value of a human
existence. Jimmie's criteria were: home, hearth, wife, land.
Those who possessed these had beatitude unchallengeable.
Other men had accidental, random life. Nothing better.

Aimed for beatitude, then, he called on the Department of
Agriculture office in Muswellbrook.

There were two white clerks quarrelling behind an oak
counter. One of them spoke upper-class English.

"Federate all you like," he was saying, "but if you do,
New South Wales will be flooded with cheap produce from
Queensland and cheap furniture from Victoria. The West Aus-
tralians and Tasmanians will never vote for union, anyhow.
They know just how they'd fare against the stronger States."

It wasn't Jimmie's argument: he wanted a leaflet on what
wood should go into fencing.

"It worked for Canadians," the local boy said. "Yer can't say it didn't work for the Americans."

"Ah, didn't the United States have trouble enforcing federation? Would you like a civil war and thousands of dead?"

"It'd never happen here. Could yer imagine Australians shooting at Australians?"

"I could imagine people who are mean-hearted, narrow and uncultivated committing every conceivable brutality. If the cap fits . . . And you seem to forget, my friend, that there's no such thing as an Australian. Except in the imaginations of some poets and at the editorial desk of the *Bulletin*."

"No such thing as an Australian?"

"Not in the political sense. Not in the sense in which there are Belgians or Germans or Frenchmen. . . ."

"Or your indomitable bloody breed!"

"Or Englishmen," the Englishman agreed. "Here there are only New South Welshmen, Victorians, Queenslanders, Vandemonians and so on. But there is no such thing as an Australian. The only true Australians are—"

At that moment he noticed Jimmie waiting at the counter.

"—the aborigines," he murmured.

The Australian too adverted to Jimmie.

"Jacko?" he called. "He's an honest poor bastard but he's nearly extinct."

"And, surprisingly, that is the work of those you so fancifully call Australians."

"It's a hard country. Lower ways of life give way to higher. Your crowd believe that. Look what yer done to the Irish and the poor bloody Highlander. My grandfather was a poor bloody Highlander. Christ, yer gave them a chance, didn't yer? So poor bloody black Jacko's gone. It's sad, but he had to go, and now there are six States that wish, without any necessary disrespect to the mother country, to make themselves into a federation and face common enemies."

"What common enemies?"

"The Asiatics. The Russian Pacific ambitions."

The Englishman sniffed. "I don't think you'll be seeing any Cossacks. I think you put too high a price on your quite unstrategic country."

"I wish we put a high enough price on it to keep out wingeing buggers like you."

"Don't you worry. I don't intend to stay here for ever. There *are* financial problems attached to going home. The fare . . ."

"When we've got a federal government, my friend, it'll pass a law to give every single wingeing bloody Pommie his fare home to England. Back to the smoke and the sun shining ten days a year and shit in the streets. Yer can have it. We'll have Federation, thank you."

The Englishman pretended to sort papers, but the Department of Agriculture wasn't getting its value out of either of them today.

"All I can say is that we've had a unitary system of government since the Saxons and it doesn't seem to have done us any harm."

This appeal to Saxon kings, to a deep past, to strata of common-sense government, to an imperial apogee, could raise an ambivalence in the consciousness of Australians, who were —yet were not—of that profound Britannic inheritance. To say it more clearly, it could make them peevish.

"Yer got by at the price of tyranny and the price of slaughtered Scots and Irishmen. Not to mention the poor fucking Indians."

"Come now," said the Englishman. "Language!"

"And what about the Boers? Yer want to fight them. Actually want to. Yer bringing it on, no matter what the papers say. That lecturer from the Fabian Society says England actually bloody wants the war. Then yer'll want all the poor bloody Australians and New Zealanders and Indians to enlist. The first Australian who gets a bullet through him'll be delighted to know there's no such thing as an Australian."

"Goodness, your attitude to England *is* inflammatory. What a pity you've never been there."

"What a pity you didn't fuckingwell stay there!"

The Englishman went on palely stacking leaflets.

"We shall see when Mr Parr rises from his bed of influenza, we shall see what he thinks about insulting a fellow officer of the Department before a visitor."

"In front of a visitor? *Jacko* over there? Mr Parr'll kick

17

yer arse in for wasting time. With his No. 9 arch-support boot from Anthony Hordern's, he'll kick yer bloody arse in."

The Englishman stamped his foot. His hands were full of handbills, entitled *Feed-Crops for the Dairy Farmer*, which trembled.

"I won't tolerate this, in front of a visitor. You will kindly serve the visitor or I shall place a complaint in memorandum form on Mr Parr's desk."

"Yer can place your memorandum on Mr Parr's desk or do any other bloody thing with it that suggests itself."

"Carmichael!"

The Federationist shrugged and strolled across to the counter.

"Yair, Jacko?"

"I want t' know about fences, boss, what yer got to do to 'em before yer put 'em in the ground. I got this contract, yer see boss, an' I want t' do a fuckin' good job."

"No language in here!"

"Beg pardon, boss."

"I mean, that's a word the glorious English created. Sometimes they do what the word suggests. Mainly to choir boys. Anyhow, it's not to be stolen by sepoys, gyppoes or boongs. You understand, Jacko?"

"I'm recording every word, Carmichael," the Englishman murmured at the rear of the office.

"I mean, Jacko, what would yer say of a New Zealand Maori or a Canadian redskin who walked into town and told them he wanted to fuckingwell know about fencing?"

Jimmie Blacksmith knew the joke that was afoot, felt a flush of collegiate friendship towards the rebel youth.

"I'd say he was a fuckin' foulmouth, boss."

The clerk hooted with joy. Jimmie let the corners of his mouth twitch ever so slightly, and his dark eyes were alight.

"Get out!" the acting office-chief was screaming. "Get out of here, you black layabout!"

Even as Jimmie began to leave, Carmichael had produced an appropriate leaflet, as if from nowhere.

"Here yer are, Jacko, here's all about fence posts. There're a lot of hardwoods round here don't need much treating or any at all, just put 'em in as they are. Anyhow, read this. Yer do read, don't yer?"

"Yair, I read, boss."

Carmichael watched him go with what seemed genuine regret.

Jimmie Blacksmith ran downstairs laughing, to the street where commercial purpose moved whites up and down the pavements with frowns of dignified intent on them. Adjusting his face to match this high mood, he stepped out to walk amongst them.

It is hard to dig post holes. You must spear the soil with an iron, seven-foot digger, again and again, weakening the nape-muscles of bull earth. When you strike sub-surface shale the iron haft jolts blisters on your palm, and soon concusses them wide and open. The new skin that then grows will be tougher, if your hands are already harsh, as Jimmie's were.

He slept in Healy's hayshed, presuming permission, coming after dark, leaving before dawn. Two meals a day were his ration. Damper and butter at breakfast, bacon and etceteras at sunset. At noon he had a drink of tea.

After a week he had post-and-railed a hundred yards. Such fast work didn't quite accord with Healy's mental budgeting.

Boundary-riding on a big splay-footed grey, Healy stopped to measure at random the distance between two of Jimmie's fence posts.

"That isn't so bad at all," he murmured, but as if Jimmie were undermining him.

3

O N SATURDAY night he went to a party up the river at a blacks' camp called Verona. He drank little—alien ambitions had made him a drinker of moderation.

He lay down with a scrawny gin called Florence but found that the preliminaries of copulation sent her into a whooping spasm.

But it was, for other reasons, a bad night and a bad place full of miserable omen. White voices could be heard as burlap door-flaps were flung open. Shrieking welcomes were sung to the white phallus, powerful demolisher of tribes. Florence barked and barked and dredged blood from beneath her lips.

He turned home in the small hours, not wanting to see Verona's Sunday sunrise.

Early the next dawn, as he neared Healy's gate and saw the pastures frosted solid, silver and blue, he was pleased to have exchanged them for the sourness of Sunday morning in Verona. In a corner of his front paddock, Healy, suited, but his russet-grey head bare, was talking to a neighbour dressed similarly for church.

On the homestead track Mrs Healy waited in the dray for her kingly husband to be finished. They were off to Mass in Merriwa or perhaps some closer Irish church in a clearing.

"Papists are not to be stoned but pitied," Mrs Neville had said once.

20

Yet Mrs Healy wore better clothes than Mrs Neville: a coat of blue velour, wide-sleeved but tight at the hips. After skinny Florence, Jimmie Blacksmith felt the appeal of those full hips; stood frankly eyeing the woman in a dewy corner of the road.

"Papists confess their sins to a priest," Mrs Neville had said, "as if there were a mediator other than Christ, as if some Irish priest could mediate between God and us."

Jimmie wished impossibly that Mrs Healy might stray with him when he became a recognizable man, an owner of things. And whoever wanted to mediate was welcome.

The Healys meanwhile had an uphill ride to Mass; downhill all the way home. What was it like to travel with Healy? Whenever Jimmie saw Mrs Healy she sat round-shouldered and had an aura of being delicate. Her lips, which were really quite fat, accumulated in the middle in a square pout of acquiescence. Her eyes were distant. She may have been very stupid or very modest. It didn't matter; arrogant at dawn after lank Florence, Jimmie deliberately chose her, though he knew the choice was an act of fantasy.

What he had done, without understanding it, was to elect her to the stature of ideal landowner's-wife. It was not simply a matter of her being full and ripe: he could not have been so potently stirred by aspects so directly sexual. But combine these with her impassive air, her peculiar way of sitting still in the dray and breathing out into the morning a vapour of worship and submission for her husband—and you had something that appealed to all Jimmie's lusts. In a second she had become a symbol, a state of blessedness, far more than a woman. It could almost be said that he did not choose her as a woman at all, rather as an archetype.

In the corner of his glistening property, Healy laughed to his neighbour and went to join his wife.

Jimmie Blacksmith did a hundred and fifty yards that week, and Healy, in shock, handed over five shillings advance.

Jimmie went to another party at Verona but liked it less. His half-caste girl, called Gay, though not as sick as Florence, had a bad cough. A lunatic gaiety shook the girl and infested the town; and when Jimmie left after midnight, horses and even a dray were tethered two or three at a time to a tree

21

at the edge of the camp. All the white lust from the town of Merriwa.

He was home in time to see Mrs Healy come out of doors in her Mass coat.

To Jimmie, who did not know Irishmen, it was a surprise that Healy should take the finished fence as an insult and insist on short-changing him.

"But it oughter be twelve shillin' more, boss," Jimmie protested when the account was settled.

"I'm not denyin' it. Two quid's all yore gettin'. There's twelve of dem posts three inches out. One of dem by more 'an four inches."

"Not by my tape, boss."

Healy's face became blank: a big-featured, militant pallor Jimmie would see overtake the faces of other Celtic penny-pinchers.

At the apex of a silence deliberately built, white cockatoos descended on Healy's tree-tops in a tribe and began chattering. Jimmie felt grateful to them.

"My tape that counts," Healy said equably at last. But Jimmie knew that if he were contradicted, there would be sudden havoc. He put his money into his pocket.

"Well, posts is solid, boss, rails cut good. Kin yer give me a ref'rence?"

"Bejesus, ye're a fussy bloody black. What d'yer need rif'rences for? A job in a bank?"

"So I kin show it t'other people wantin' fences done."

Healy's laugh could not have been understood unless you knew that at its heart stood a primitive algebra. It had cost Healy's father a great outlay of rigor to keep two acres of stony earth in Sligo. To retain therefore a thousand acres of beneficent slopes in the new world would take a massive exercise in harshness.

"I haven't got me writin' glasses," said Healy. "And I want to see yer off by ten in the mornin'."

Cunning, humble, Jimmie persisted.

"Kin I git a ride into Merriwa with yer, Mr Healy? I gor a lot of things t' carry."

"I'm not goin' to Merriwa tomorrer."

"I bin thinkin' yer might, it bein' Friday."

"I don't need yer to think for me. I'll ask yer when I want yer to do me thinkin'."

"Yair. Well . . ."

But Jimmie was at last stung by the mystery: that a wondrous landowner should need to degrade him.

"Yair. No ref'rence 'cause yer can't bloody write."

The pallor returned to Healy; the strange horn-mad pallor and stillness of the mouth. Of course it was the truth. Jimmie had seen Healy call his wife to read the invoices for goods delivered from Muswellbrook or Merriwa. Jimmie had seen him force his splayed fingers to make an arduous signature. The nuns who had taught Mrs Healy writing and humility had never seen Healy.

Healy hit Jimmie. The impact was demeaning: Jimmie's thin legs flew from beneath him and there he was, instantly on his shoulder blades.

It did not hurt so very much.

The next forenoon Jimmie was travelling west with his gear when the Healys, their dissimilar eyes averted, passed him on the road. He found himself swearing to possess her to depths that were probably not in her.

It was strange how she had become inherent to his programme.

4

UP AND DOWN the valley, Jimmie took other work, and word reached Brentwood that he was making sums of money. Lazy members of his totem would associate any task like fencing with sums of money. To Jackie Smolders, for example, it occurred that he should cross the Divide and ask for his part—a maternal uncle's part, supreme in Mungindi lore—of Jimmy's pay.

But Jackie mistrusted the mountains. There were fables about their formation that alarmed him.

There was one fortnight when Jimmie seemed taken over by a bad spirit, lassitude and submission he could not account for. Obsessed, he spent the time at Verona, frightened by the obsession. And Verona frightened him too. It seemed that an eye—God's eye—had ceased to see Verona squarely. The image ran like an ulcer at the edges.

At night the candle-light was fragmented, and shattered the silhouettes of boys from town and lubras dancing out their death.

One evening a hut lit up and began to burn with a festive intensity. It belonged to a fat lady whose friends held her back from entering this purest thing in Verona, this diverse squalor refined to the clean unity of a tongue of fire.

"All me things!" she kept screaming. "All me things! All me keepsakes!"

24

For a second Jimmie Blacksmith would willingly have burned Verona off the map.

Sometimes too he would ask a girl, "Wot's yer animal-spirit, eh, yer black bitch? I bin killin' a lot of animals lately. What animal's got yer soul, eh?"

They didn't like that sort of chat. But he was the one in genuine alarm.

One evening he was woken. It was a Saturday and he had drunk a lot of bad sherry early in the afternoon.

"Get up, Jimmie," one of the anonymous people of Verona asked him. "Harry Edwards gone and stuck 'im a whitey wiv a knife."

"The whitey much hurt?"

"Hurt? 'Im fuckin' dead, Jimmie. Git up. Yer got t'help bury 'im."

"Yer kin bury 'im yerselves."

The Mungindi were able to handle their aitches, the natives of Verona only some, but a rough sort of politeness made Jimmie copy them.

"We let yer have our woman. Yer help us bury this bloody whitey."

It was a bitter night. To step from the animal-warm hut into the midnight was like walking on to a knife.

There were a dozen men in Harry Edwards's hut, all wide-eyed at the lovely dead white boy with his well-sown hare-lip. Blood was still surging out of his upper belly as from something living. Jimmie had seen the face somewhere, in one of the towns.

The wound bled so plentifully onto the earth floor that Sally, wife to Harry, began to pack her chairs onto the stinking bed in the corner.

Someone said that the boy could be best carried a distance in a blanket, by the four corners. Sally replied that she didn't want to have a good blanket ruined beyond repair.

" 'E was orright," Harry explained. " 'E go and lie down with Sally."

"Don't do much, 'e don't," Sally said.

" 'E wake up and don't know where 'e is. He says we tricked 'im 'ere to sleep with filthy gin, I ask 'im for a little cash. 'E go bloody mad. Yellin'. 'E start breakin' 'em Sally things. I got to stop 'im. I git meat knife."

"Jesus, yer made a big hole in 'im, Harry."

"He with mates?" Jimmie Blacksmith asked. Because if the boy had come with friends, they might begin to search Verona for him.

"They hang Harry certain as all shit," Harry said. "But I didn't see no friends."

They took one of the blankets from Sally's bed to wrap the boy in. Then another just for carrying, so that Sally lost two. An old man went ahead with a storm lantern, then the eight or nine carriers and a boy dragging a eucalyptus bough. The earth was uneven but the corpse light. They could carry him one-handed, sometimes bringing their other hand to bear when the balance shifted.

"What animal's got yer soul, eh?" Jimmie had asked black girls.

When the corpse jolted it was with a slick wet sound and everyone averted his eyes and mind from the bad omen of blood too copious for the blanket to take in.

"Here," someone said. Dubious authority: for this place was close to the camp. Someone would have to move it on the first quiet night. Places were infected by the bad portent of blood. Even places where the New South Wales Commissioner for Aboriginal Affairs said, "Here shall be a camp"; naming it Verona in whimsical hope of justice as fine as Shakespeare's. Even such places as that were infected. Those in the know would tend, while sleeping, to suffer from the gory omens of the dead boy.

"Here," the voice said, anxious to be safe quickly, as all of them were.

Between them they managed to dig a hole two feet deep. In the dark they confused each other with meaningless advice.

The boy they wrapped up with all the evil auguries of his blood neat in Sally's blanket.

"What animal's got yer soul, eh?"

Not only did Jimmie feel that Verona, its chaos of black-white meanness, was off God's globe, if God had a globe. But worse, that they had hurriedly buried the animal of their

26

true totem without propitiatory rites and out of a necessity that should not have arisen.

He had no family there and no woman he loved; and so, except for one other visit a year later, that was the last time he went to Verona.

For he was a hybrid. If he had been tribal man, love would have been written into the order of his day. All his acts would have been acts of solemn and ritual preference. Love would have been in their fibre.

But having chosen to grub and build as whites do, he knew that love was a special fire that came down from God. A mere visitor. After a brief hectic season, it extended itself more soberly to your children and the boundaries of your land.

Suspended between the loving tribal life and the European rapture from on high called falling in love (at which even Mr Neville had hinted), Jimmie Blacksmith held himself firm and soundly despised as many people as he could.

But there is little enough interest in a man who loves nobody. In fact, Jimmie was surprised to find that he loved his half-brother Morton, who was innocent and loyal, who came to see Jimmie because he hated the thought of kinsmen lost amidst strangers.

In the time between Verona and Morton's arrival, Jimmie Blacksmith had worked for a number of farmers, who had cautioned and paid him in the Healy style.

Now he had taken a contract with an old Scot called Claude Lewis.

Lewis mistrusted Morton, who had Dulcie's flippancy. As old Lewis stumped about with a yard-stick, breathing sinusitically through a soiled moustache, Mort would double with laughter, would sit down on a tree-stump and quiver at some quaintness in the man.

"What's worryin' blackie, o'er thire?"

"Nothin', Mr Lewis. He's jist a boy."

"Yer nae gunner turn me property into a blacks' camp, are ye?"

"No, boss. No blacks' camp."

How these farmers feared the tribal intentions of the black man.

"Cut it out, Mort," Jimmie would scream. "Give it a rest."

Lewis would snort into his greyed slack moustache that had once been ginger and buoyant.

"Still canna see what he's laughin' at."

When Lewis was gone, Jimmie would reproach Morton; but sometimes he too would be infected by laughter.

"The whitey he made me," he said once, "he must have been solemn bastard. Or somethink."

Morton had found him early on in the Lewis contract. It had been a hot day in December 1898, and Jimmie had felt unease the moment he saw a black stick wading in the ghost-vapours where the road took a crest at least a mile away.

He sensed the stick was kin of his. It proved to be thin kin, with big child-like teeth, chanting wild affection in Mungindi plainsong:

> *Breed of Emu-Wren, see your breed coming*
> *Shouting the day's joy as you*
> *Shout the day's welcome.*
> *I sing my welcomes to you too*
> *As I take you by the shoulders*
> *And my hands clap,*
> *Recognizing eyes, and beards*
> *Jutted with smiling.*

Though he could not stop himself smiling, Jimmie Blacksmith was wary of the song and Morton's love. Therefore he made it clear to Mort that he allowed him to stay for reasons of commerce rather than of tribal section.

"If yer couldn' work like yer do, I'd boot yer black arse out of here."

It was, in fact, all nervousness with Mort, and a desire to give a kind of welcome.

Such welcomes Lewis wouldn't accept. The Scot found fault all the time, fictional faults with his yardstick—cannier, he implied, than Jimmie's tape. There were threats that Jimmie's poor wages would be cut to a point at which he would not be able to buy food for Mort and himself.

Jimmie, once more, did not know Scottish history, or reasons why people called Lewis should relish so their ferocious bookkeeping.

One morning Jimmie and Mort Blacksmith simply walked away from Lewis's.

Over the hills, in Scone, they got casual work from a squatter. Mort got a reputation as a horse-breaker. His talent arose from his ignorance and lack of fear of wild horses and his willingness to believe the best of animals. His big toes hooked into the horse's belly, his thin boy's body jolted madly up and down the spine. Of course, he giggled without ceasing. In the end even the horse would be bemused by that.

The once or twice he was thrown he would lie belly-first in the dirt and then roll on his back, one leg crooked like a tickled dog, hooting and whooping glee.

"All the bloody time laugh, Mort, it's no good."

"Why?"

"Yard boss say bloody stupid boong. . . . Next thing yer know about yer git yer marchin' orders."

But the laughter persisted, and had a hint about it that Mort's joke was very private and cherished for its secrecy. Whites resented such hints.

One night Jimmie had another strange experience of this endless chortling. At the blacks' camp outside Scone, he slept with a full-blood in the same room where Mort had her half-breed sister. The symmetry of the situation was not planned, yet might have accounted why, half-way through his penetration of the girl, Mort could be heard chuckling. And the girl too, as if he had passed the contagion of his joke to her with his seed.

The truth was that Mort was only seventeen, and awkward.

In the late autumn of 1899, the two brothers went home to Brentwood. In the mission station the legend was rife of the Blacksmith brothers' success in the large world.

A child who saw them called out, "Here come the rich fellers."

Tabidgi Jackie Smolders waited at Dulcie's place to receive the maternal uncle's share of their goods and money. Forty-two years, but an ancient man. His status had not stopped

29

him from drinking sherry-and-varnish. As a result his beard had fallen out in tufts.

"Yer don't want t' think us Blacksmiths rich boys," Mort told him. "I got fifteen bob and some beef and flour."

Tabidgi was visibly disappointed at Morton's pathetic inventory. Nonetheless he took what Mort had and distributed it amongst Emu-Wren, as much as distribution was feasible.

The ambitions of Emu-Wren being blatantly alcoholic this chilly day, Jimmie Blacksmith made a sour face at the tribal system itself. Mort, less complex, less undermined, could not be dissuaded from simple, giggling joy at being home.

"How yer off, Jimmie?"

There was a crowd to see Jimmie Blacksmith give up his fortune to his kin. To them one was identified, endowed, augmented, in the giving.

"How'm I off?"

"Yer got much, Jimmie?"

"Much what?"

Everyone was frowning.

"Christ!" Jimmie screamed and took notes and silver from his pocket and pelted them at the dust.

It was a great loss to him. It was the measure of his experience of the world, his £2 15s. It should not have come from him so easily. Now he had only the things that swagmen have, flour, beef, tobacco.

In the shock of having done what he had done he went indoors in Dulcie's hut and lay on a mattress with his face to the wall. Where bark had shorn off, a piece of tin was hammered to an upright, but free at one end. It trembled delicately with the wind—Dulcie would have to see to something more adequate than that. *Nammonia*—to use Dulcie's word—got in at places like that. *Nammonia* had killed Wilf.

Dulcie followed him inside.

"Tired?"

"Yair. We have a gab a little later, eh, Dulcie?"

"Orright."

She pottered about, crooning.

> *Child of mine, spill what tears you have*
> *As you grow to be a man*

Your tears will grow to be
Rivers in high flood.

"Tabidgi made Wilf nice cross," she called. "The parson say his prayers real nice for poor bloody old Wilf. He was awful sick. He was always talkin' about findin' you, about goin' off. He use t' call yer name out when he had his fits."

For the rest of his home-coming day, Jimmie Blacksmith slept off his confusion. As he slept, Tabidgi selected men to sneak into town for booze.

He stayed two days only at Brentwood, sleeping a great deal and in a kind of languor. Sometimes he was awoken by lurching songs—all his money going up in bad music.

He found out too that Dulcie had remarried: that was a detail Dulcie had not mentioned. The groom was a half-breed half-wit who chuckled like Mort, yet far more vacantly, far more quietly. He sat in corners studiously spitting bloody phlegm into a peach tin. You could have fitted a cricket ball between the sagging ganglions at the base of his throat.

Of course, Jimmie vacated the marriage mattress and slept wrapped in a blanket, slept strenuously, sapped and in shock. Perhaps in what anthropologists would call cultural shock later on, too late to help Emu-Wren.

Now Dulcie was old and slept with dying men. The maternal uncle was a moulting drunkard. Dottie had consumption and a husband who beat her. Emu-Wren was hawking up its living tissue.

He should have been glad but was unconsolable. When Dulcie brought him food he turned his head into a corner.

"You paley bastard make me sad," she said. But she was not desolate. Her brain sat warmly behind its tribal vapours. And booze too. One night she would fall down drunk and frost would grow over her. A swift *nammonia* would see her safe into Brentwood cemetery.

5

$\mathbf{J}$IMMY BLACKSMITH left early and took an unexpected direction. Since his name now connoted someone who had crossed the Divide in the east, he went west. Not north-west along the tribal river Marooka. Not Marooka because there were towns on all its fords to drop rumours of him south to Brentwood. But beyond the Castlereagh, where the squatters were full of heart again after the long drought, there was a plague of red kangaroos. The pastoralists paid up to a shilling a tail for kangaroos shot on their property.

Leaving Brentwood he was bare-footed and his feet crunched the stiff frost, and the whining of dogs steamed round his legs. Somewhere in the camp an early-riser was hacking wood.

He had only essentials with him, and his axe and razor-sharp wedges. But he was on his way to the true station country, where money was plentiful and the squatters' wives had servants; "nice girls off stations", as Mrs Neville had said.

One morning, he felt sure, he would wake up "Mr Blacksmith". Drily, gutturally, he sang a song out of the white dances they used to have in Muswellbrook. His intentions were exemplary; it was delight to find oneself a just man.

He had cleared Mudgee, pleased to have put a big town between Tabidgi Jackie Smolders and himself.

Then he met a mounted trooper travelling east from Wellington. The policeman's broad heavy bay held its nostrils wide, stimulated by the day, and the officer himself seemed to be attempting to match this bravura by riding one-handed with his right fist on his hip. Lazily, he shortened rein and halted by Jimmie Blacksmith.

"Wot yer got in the bag, Jacko?"

"Me tools of trade." Jimmie held the mouth of his bag wide.

"Axe, wedges," the trooper recited. "Wot trade is it?"

"Fencin', boss."

"P'liceman, 'e thinks yer bloody steal all them."

"No boss. I buy 'em with contract money from Mr Healy near Merriwa."

"Merriwa?"

"Yair, constable."

"I'm stationed at Merriwa. Me name's Senior Constable Farrell. Yer watch out fer me if ever yer git on the booze, Jacko!"

"Orright."

"I jest took a man t' Wellington t' git hanged, Jacko. A man about yer own age. He killed a sixteen-year-old girl in Wellington, just because she had his bun in the oven. What d' yer think of that sort of behaviour, Jacko?"

"Bloody disgraceful, boss."

"I should say so. Soon he'll meet Mr Hyberry? Yer know Mr Hyberry, Jack?"

"No, boss."

"A famous gentleman, Mr Hyberry. A butcher from Balmain, and public hangman as well. He's a scholar, Mr Hyberry. One of the honours of me life, meeting him. Where yer off to now, Jack?"

"West."

Farrell raised his eyebrows at finding a black who knew his cardinal points.

"Can't stand bloody Brentwood," Jimmie further confessed.

"Kin yer track, Jacko?"

"Yair, I kin track."

"Go ahead and track."

That was easy. The west crawled with rabbits. Their spoor, scarcely broken by his own morning tracks and the trooper's,

33

were all over the road. His finger traced padmarks along the edge of the road and into tussocks on the verge. Somebody's boundary fence ran to his left and above him to his right was a hillock with three ancient peppermint trees. Here was a camp-site for bullock drivers, but the earth beneath had been tortuously mined by pestilential rabbits.

There were so many clear tracks across the frost that Jimmy Blacksmith thought the trick hardly worth doing, and turned back. But there was Farrell's horse bouncing and snorting, steam rising from its croup, and Farrell himself seemed still to be willing to be impressed. So Jimmy shrugged and went on.

Rabbit was of course no one's totem—an imported animal, everyone's fair game. Minute shifts in the lie of grass and twig and fallen leaf led Jimmie Blacksmith across the lacing of other tracks to a burrow.

"I can't see nothing," Farrell called.

"It's a rabbit hole, boss."

Jimmie began to dig up its secret geography with his axe. At last three animals broke from the earth between his legs and Constable Farrell, without smiling, shot one through the shoulders with his dragoon pistol.

When Jimmie had fetched it, Farrell tied the little corpse to his saddle with string. "Give him t' Mrs Public House in Mudgee," he explained. "I been told t' recruit a tracker for Merriwa. Don't want any of them lazy boongs from Verona. What about yerself? Seven and six a week. Tucker, horse. Yer sleep in the stable. No boots. Yer kin git 'em out of the seven and six if you want t' pretend yer a gentleman. But I tell yer it isn't any kind of lazy black's job. Yer look after all the horses—three troopers' and yer own, and yer cut the firewood for the station and the residence."

Saying nothing, Jimmie began to hanker for the work. It must be a good reference, to have worked for the police. In a police station he would be fortified against his demanding kinsmen. He watched the brightly wounded animal. Its back legs shivered ever so little.

"Well, d'yer want t' be a p'liceman? Cut a figure with the gins in Verona?"

"Seven an' six ain't so bad," said Jimmie.

34

"Orright. But yer got to be at Merriwa by this day next week. I got other darkies in mind and if yer don't come, Jacko, yer kin go begging."

"Orright, boss."

Senior Constable Farrell rolled away comfortably on his mount. Like everyone else, he knew that a black could walk twenty miles a day, day after day. If only he had a boot in the arse to help him along.

But when they gave him his uniform, Jimmie Blacksmith understood his mistake. The blue coat was a giant's, the cap loose, the trousers knifed him in the crutch. He had taken a florid foreign oath to Victoria and was now on the books as a tracker, a comic abo in some other black's clothes.

"Roll up the sleeves," Constable Farrell suggested without interest. "Give 'em all a wash if yer want to. Ole Bunyal was a good tracker, but a dirty old bastard. Wot yer want us t' call yer? Ole Bunyal got registered under his abo name, yer know. Not that we care either way. Only we have t' send all the papers to Sydney. T' make it official. So wot yer want us to call yer?"

Jimmie told him, J. Blacksmith.

"Is that so?"

"Yair."

He was allowed to sit against the wall while they waited for a junior constable to come and show him his duties in detail. At the desk Farrell had begun attending to the paperwork. His public service pen whimpered his signature across the secret paper which senior constables were permitted to make marks on. Once he looked up.

"Yer a missionary black, Jimmie?"

"Yair."

"I kin always tell a missionary black. Bunyal wasn't one. Mind yer, a bloody good tracker."

Jimmie's face prickled. He had been a policeman for half an hour yet now wanted to commit murder. He was more officially a black now than Tabidgi or Mort: a registered, accredited, uniformed black man; more deeply, more damagingly black than ever.

There was, in fact, so much to keep him busy that he could

35

drug the sense of his folly with the strong drug of a demi-military existence. He had three mounts to see to, cavalry saddles to clean, weapons to maintain, fires to feed, many fires, since Merriwa was high and frosty. Three times a day he cut wood, and ran messages for the junior senior constable, who was married (unlike Farrell) and thought that he, therefore, should occupy the police residence. The balance was adjusted, the junior senior constable thought, by using Jimmie for private convenience, such as for fetching meat from the butcher's.

Sometimes he rode on duty up the pass to that camp of bad omen where the white boy had been knifed and inadequately buried a year before. But no one in Verona seemed to recognize Jimmie in his unfamiliar uniform.

There was little tracking to do, but whenever a constable had to arrest a black, Jimmie was expected to accompany in case persuasion was needed, or a show of strength.

Senior Constable Farrell's passion was boar-hunting. Very few other people between whom contempt existed could have achieved such a unity of expertise as did Farrell and Jimmie Blacksmith on the track of a boar.

Then occurred the come-uppance that brought Jimmie's police career to a head.

The postmaster's son, driven by conscience, came nervously to Farrell. He hadn't wanted to insult a respected family, he told Farrell (the statement sounding rehearsed and creaky), but a boy called Jack Fisher, who had vanished a year ago, had been drinking after hours in the Prince Albert in Merriwa the night he disappeared and had said about ten that he meant to ride out to Verona for some black velvet.

Farrell knew that at the tail-end of sprees in town whites often took off for Verona to lie with the gins. There was many a town elder who had reason to cringe at the sight of some trachoma-eyed half-caste child who had his jaw or nose or forehead. It was always the white man's good luck that the lubra knew nothing so obscene as blackmail. If you were an alderman who had once gone with a gin, the worst you had to fear was that the woman might call out a greeting to you in the main street, even within sight of the superior architecture of the municipal offices or School of Arts.

"G'day, Eddie," she might sing in a musical monotone, one third ironic, one third resigned, one third heinously innocent.

For their part, men never boasted about their love-making with gins. Perhaps the sport was too easy for that. And no one willingly admitted that there was an especial pull in the easy, slack-mouthed lubras. Certainly they provided a free whore-house just beyond the limits; but everyone suspected that there were degenerates who actually preferred black flesh, whatever economies were involved, and men were pointed out in whispers whose taste for black flesh had so sapped them that they no longer wanted any white.

Now Jack Fisher's father, undertaker, free-holder, Merriwa Croesus, had died and could not be hurt, said the post-master's son.

Feeling no danger, Jimmie Blacksmith in fact exulted that the question of the dead white boy, aching with inconclusion, had been raised again.

He would be savage, a regular vengeance in his too-big blue coat, to the guilty of Verona.

Farrell too was especially enjoying himself.

"We enquired of yer at the time," he said grandly, "and yer mentioned nothink about the darkies' camp."

"I thought it'd be too much for old Fisher. If he knew Jack had disappeared in that manner."

"And yer were out there too, and didn't want t' git yerself into trouble from yer father."

"No, that wasn't the reason."

"Were yer out there?"

"No."

"Come on, it's obvious."

The boy's freckled hand pinched his forehead.

"Orright."

Farrell said, "This is serious. Yer knew he'd gone fuckin' gins and yer didn't tell us."

"I was worried about old Fisher's health."

"Did he go out there regular? I mean, did he have a regular gin?"

"No. No. I was one of his best mates and I don't know that he went out to Verona much."

"The gin he had that night. Wot was her name?"

37

"I don't know. He went off to another hut from me. Later I waited where the horses were tethered, but I kept falling asleep."

"Ah, wear yerself out, did yer?"

"So I thought Jack must be making a night of it, so I rode back home."

"And the darkies took his harness and ate his horse, I s'pose?"

"I don't know. He should've been safe there."

"Well, he wasn't. But we'll find him. And then yer can tell Merriwa all about courting gins."

"But I've got a fiancée."

"Then yer better get her in the family way. Then she can't back out."

So Farrell's viciousness went on consecrating itself to the sacredness of Jack Fisher's right not to get his vitals punctured in Verona.

Of course, Jimmie knew, Farrell was not normal and had once begun to caress him, before deciding it might be bad for authority. Farrell enjoyed putting terror into lusty boyhood.

Jimmie himself was in a vindictive state of mind. The Verona people were to be punished for their vulnerability. There was a lust in him to punish the race through the man who had done the knifing. Near the dry tip of Jimmie's tongue the man's name wavered. Harry Edwards was the name.

Farrell armed himself and Jimmie had the horses waiting at the front of the station. Both nursing private excitement, they rode through the town's quiet midday. Small boys came running to the wire fence of the school.

> *Black, black,*
> *Dressed in a sack,*
> *Leave our town*
> *And don't come back!*

Farrell led Jimmie on into a dark seeping quietness, myrtle and red cedar, capable of drowning anyone's doggerel.

But in Verona, too, children ran behind the horses, hooting

Jimmie for his uniform. All the women showed up in their doorways, ululating as if the visit were an honour, and giggling. Men began to run. Even the ones indoors rucked past their chortling women and ran.

"C'mon, Jimmie," Farrell said. He nudged his horse into a gallop and had a bludgeon in his hands. First he caught an old man and knocked him down. Then a much younger man, who seemed to be a mesh of black-pink fingers raised against Farrell's blackjack. Just in time to snatch Farrell's flung reins, Jimmie caught up. He found the bludgeon handed to him.

"Go and git a few more, Jimmie."

Farrell had dismounted and begun to compose the two men he had caught, holding one of them with each hand.

Jimmie could have led Farrell straight to the grave, yet that would be silly. For he and Farrell had punishment to distribute, and *that* should be allowed to take its time.

But once he entered the forest he found it hard to turn in the same small circles as the fleeing men. A man broke across his front, a drinking man like Jackie Smolders, with grey hair around his ears. Reaching low, Jimmie cracked him at the base of the skull. The drinking man circled, clasping his ears. A resonance of another sort ran up the bludgeon and along Jimmie Blacksmith's arm. He felt lordly drunk, but was less deft with a second man.

In the camp, Farrell was ranting and even the dogs were silent.

"Young whitefeller dead here. 'E die in Verona. A year back. 'Im maybe buried round the place. Close. Bloody darkie too lazy bury 'im far away. Where yer bury 'im? Eh? Yer tell p'liceman Farrell or p'liceman Farrell knock 'im bloody black head off."

"Dead?" the old man was weeping. "What yer mean 'im dead?"

"I mean 'im maybe got killed by blackfeller."

"Whitefeller killed?" The young man was trying to understand. One of his ears was bleeding.

"Yair. I told yer. 'Im maybe killed by some bloody Verona black."

All the women at their doors began shrilling.

At this stage, the murderer's name had become an almost involuntary spasm of Jimmie's tongue and he could not prevent himself taking a risk. He placed a hand on the shoulder of one of the men he had brought back.

"This feller, 'e say Harry Edwards have fight with young whitefeller."

The man was too bludgeoned to deny it.

"Kill whitefeller?"

"Put bloody knife in 'im."

"Where this one Harry Edwards live?"

As everyone tenuously conscious pointed out a hovel of bark and clap-board, Jimmie Blacksmith hated them for their innocence, for not being able to dominate even the clumsiness of Farrell.

Sally Edwards was still on her doorstep, looking with a detachment at Farrell, ready to moan or shrill or giggle with all her sisters of the chorus.

"Harry Edwards yer man?"

"Yair." Sally covered her mouth and writhed with laughter at the idea. Perhaps Farrell would have been less amazed if he had ever met Morton Blacksmith.

"What's yer own name?"

"Sally," she said. Jimmie could see the terror helpless beneath unceasing laughter.

"Sally, where yer man 'im husband?"

"'Im lazy bastard." She choked on her hilarity. "'E go sleep Freddie's place."

Farrell went to wake 'im lazy bastard, Harry. Meanwhile, though he had been drained and half-asleep a year ago, Jimmy Blacksmith knew where the boy's grave was. Even though the body had probably been moved for fear of its evil influence, the removal would have been much later and the marks of the low-hung load would very likely be legible in the undergrowth. Yet he must not make the mistake of vaulting ahead of Farrell's stolid procedures.

These, within an hour, had lain Harry Edwards on his stomach. Jimmie's blood leapt and was tantalized by the whole affair, and Jimmie knew how obscene that was, but was lost in his passion. All the nervous lubras were snickering and chanting when Farrell decided that prone Harry needed water and sent a young man to get it. Off went the boy, with a hobble of terrible biddability.

A person could see that Farrell was gratified by the progress of the case. He would have felt undermined if presented with too early a grave. But Jimmie was so restless that he actually went and inspected it.

It was later than he thought when he came out of the forest. Harry was lying in the shade of his lean-to, and Farrell was interviewing some of the ladies, who tamped laughter back down their throats with maladroit, splay-fingered hands. Sublimely hating them for the wounds they so childishly contracted, Jimmie aligned himself by Farrell's side.

At last someone was willing to take them to the first grave. Where the second was, they said, they didn't know, because the man who had helped Harry make it had left Verona.

It began to rain, but the eroded tracks were clear. Harry and his assistant had carried the corpse uneconomically, side-wise, had broken and altered the history of the undergrowth. It was likely, of course, that they were drunk at the time.

Jimmie Blacksmith followed the traces for a quarter of a mile in the wet, in a forest slack-boughed, limp beneath the thick-dropped rain, pliant as the men who followed Farrell and would do any necessary digging. A tableau recurred to him, a vineyard of gallows from which hung all the inept, unfortunate race, emphatically asleep. Their limbs span in a breeze, so well had sleep invaded all their ligaments.

It'd be a good thing, Jimmie felt sure; like a white realist.

Meanwhile he kept his darkie's place so well that he found a bungled grave above a running stream that must have been quite beautiful by sunlight. The boulders it had tumbled in flood made a bastion of the place and allowed soil to accumulate to a depth.

Frightened Harry had not exploited depth sufficiently, however.

Now the men were set digging. Soon there was a stink of corpse and men warded it off with hands and groans and hysterical chuckling.

Farrell hit one of the laughers and more of them laughed,

and attained paroxysms by the time the bones appeared in their remnants of wet flesh.

Jimmie felt justified, once more knowing the emotion indecent and one that might run beyond his control; but justified. Atrocious death, the boy's and even his own, had always lain latent in Verona. Now he had somehow struck back at it.

The fact of this discovery was detailed in the sombre Sydney *Herald*, and the Sydney *Mail* wrote to Mr Farrell for a photogaph of himself and Jimmie.

"Bloody nonsense," Farrell said. "Take up too much time." But sent one of himself.

At the funeral, Jack Fisher's mother came up to Farrell, the mouth fixed in the strange leer of those who have determined to pay their debts exactly, zealously.

"I don't begrudge you, constable," she said, and gave him three hundred pounds.

"Should I inform my superiors of yer generosity, madam?" Farrell asked in an outbreak of gallantry.

He came back to the station so inflated with public regard and the minister's oratory that he made a speech of his own, about how he respected blacks that showed talent and the terms on which the white man and the black man could work together.

That these terms were not exactly reciprocal might be indicated by the fact that he gave Jimmie £2 10s. of Mrs Fisher's reward.

One night soon after, Senior Constable Farrell began to drink in the office by himself. In Farrell drunk there was no trace of fun, not even a spurious sense of fellowship. He howled and stumbled, and swore about people who had wronged him.

Harry Edwards understood the dangers in drunkenness and began chanting in terror. Jimmie could not tell what the murderer was singing in the cells; it would have been about dying among foreigners, amongst people whose totem he did not know, whose totem he had stalked and devoured.

Songs utterly unavailing to sing in a country station of the New South Wales Mounted Police.

Meanwhile, Farrell sang too—"Phelim Brady", and a song

called "Come All Ye Lachlan Men". He did not sing well or becomingly and had, in fact, taken his uniform off, song by song, jolting about the office in his drawers. His phallus became erect. Jimmie, who knew Farrell's weakness and the traditions of jailhouse sodomy, decided to escape to the stables.

As he passed the cells Harry Edwards raised his own song to a clamouring yodel.

"Mr P'liceman," he called to Jimmie. Strangely, he had not seen in this man the accomplice to last year's killing. All his congenital powers of recognition were jangled by Jimmie's European uniform.

"Yeah?" Jimmie stood still. For a mad second he thought of explaining to the man how, because he was wanton and stupid, Verona had sprung blood onto his hands.

"Away and make way for the bold Fenian men!" Farrell howled in a cracked baritone.

"Wot for yer leavin' 'im Harry to Mr Farrell?"

" 'Im Harry murder white boy."

There was no need for them to go on with the '*im* business —it was part of the police concept of how the native spoke English. For that very reason, for the sake of putting Harry at a distance, Jimmie Blacksmith kept to it.

"Yair, but Mr Farrell 'im goin' t' do somethink bad to 'im Harry."

" 'Im Harry ought t' git somethink bad done to 'im."

" 'Im Harry knife 'im white boy. But . . ." And Harry, not knowing that Jimmie Blacksmith had already heard it, told the story of how the boy, after lying with Sally, began to destroy the house.

"Still Harry got a knife got too bloody sharp edge."

"Christ, don' leave 'im Harry. Harry 'im don't want 'im Farrell muckin' round."

Jimmie Blacksmith knew that he was being exquisitely cruel and that it was bad for his soul, that it might put him closer to madness most ruinous to his ambitions.

"Why 'im Harry give 'im woman to 'im white boy?"

Harry did not understand the point.

"Whiteman 'im don't lend no one 'im wife. 'E keep her all the time, even when 'e borrow gin all the time. She lie down with 'im other man, whiteman kill 'im wife. Maybe kill 'im man too, often as not. So why yer bloody give Sally for 'im white boy ride?"

Certainly Harry tried to understand the point. His eyes glazed with the import of it.

But Jimmie Blacksmith went and rolled himself up for sleep and slept obdurately, hearing unwillingly sounds of Harry's misuse, which Harry had merited. By not understanding.

In the morning he made Farrell's tea in the big kitchen of the station residence. Beyond the window there was a benign splendour of frost and unequivocal early sunlight. The wet fences of the town ran downhill and, pitched into the bottom of the valley, the main street had a new-born look which Jimmie loved yet knew would not last much beyond nine o'clock. In a white town, Jimmie affirmed the morning as a way of disaffirming Harry Edwards.

Farrell's tea was ready and Jimmie took it to him. The senior constable was soberly asleep by the stove, between two blankets. He wore a police issue shirt and, as it proved, his breeches—very much *On Her Majesty's Service*.

Apart from a knotted look on Farrell's high forehead, there was no sign of last night's drunk, and it was only on turning to go that Jimmie saw Harry Edwards hanging from the roof of his cell. The colour of his eyes was lost in staring, popping white. A long thick tongue, loose as a broken serpent, lolled out of a mouth fixed as if for screaming.

"Harry Edwards hanged himself with his belt," Farrell informed Jimmie. "I'm going t' see the magistrate. While I'm away I want yer t' take Harry down, take his clothes off and burn 'em, wash him and wrap him up in a blanket, head and everythink. There'll have to be a inquest."

Jimmie Blacksmith detachedly took down the corpse, his mind as shut as a nurse's might be to its reek of shit and urine and seed. If he was tender at disposing the limbs, it was with the workaday tenderness one would expect of someone used to handling the dead.

The belt was new, at least by Harry Edwards's standards; the finishing still shone, there was no crack into the texture of

44

the leather. It was certainly Farrell's belt and Jimmie laid it on Farrell's blotter . . . to indicate contempt. Then he tucked Harry away in a blanket.

To the fire he made of Harry's clothes he added his own over-long coat and crutch-nipping blue trousers. The cap he left on the jailhouse bench for whoever would be Farrell's next tracker.

Then he put on his old clothes and had walked ten miles by noon.

He was twenty years old, going back over the mountains again, on the look-out for a cheap Enfield or Sharps rifle.

"Yer can't trust 'em," Farrell told the junior senior constable next day. "Yer just git one of 'em into shape and they go off on bloody walkabout."

6

NEXT NOVEMBER, beyond hot Cowra, under a high sun and by the heat-trap of the Weddin mountains, Jimmie got work as a sweeper on a shearing floor. He swept droppings and tailings.

As well, he helped the cook, a man with a strange past—so everyone said—who spoke like an educated Englishman, wore a butterfly collar, however soiled, while cooking. When he swore he said *damned* or even *deuced*. He received the *London Illustrated News* by post and knew all about Communism.

At night the shearers used to question him about the disgrace that had made him a shearers' cook in Cowra. Some thought he might have been a grammar-school master who had been accused of corrupting boys. Others imagined ruined servant-girls and other caddish situations from British melodrama. They all half-suspected that he was simply a native-born draper's assistant who put his hand into the takings; but that did not satisfy their hunger for a man of mystery, a gentleman of diverse and sporty malevolence, now brought low.

The people who owned the sheep station were called Hayes. One day Jimmie Blacksmith found the cook trying to hypnotize the Hayeses' kitchen-maid.

She was a small girl, perhaps seventeen. Her hair was lank

and thin but had a clean tone of yellow in it. Mrs Hayes, a shearer had said, got her kitchen-maids from a home for wayward girls in Sydney. But this one did not look pretty or individual enough to justify the adjective. Her face was narrow. Most of the time she fretted about the house, her mouth gaping adenoidally with the effort to serve Mrs Hayes.

Now, coming into the shearers' cookhouse, Jimmie found he had broken the cook's concentration and flustered the girl.

The cook said bitterly, "But why should you be worked on by an amateur? Here comes the witchdoctor of the shearing floor."

The girl looked sideways at Jimmie and let the beginnings of a smile turn up the corners of her bleak open mouth.

"Put a spell on the young lady, Jimmie."

Jimmie glanced at her, very angry that he should be vulnerable before such a poor woman.

"I don't go in fer that sort of stuff, Mister cook."

"Aha! Dark and deadly tribal secrets!" the cook called out like a busker at a country sideshow.

The girl risked a small restrained giggle that allied her with the cook.

"It's all nonsense, boss."

"Oh, I've hurt your feelings, Jimmie," said the cook with a secondary sort of sympathy that was only a small distance from sarcasm. "We Europeans are so poor in spirit that the best we can do is laugh at primitive people who, in my experience, always have *something*, God knows what it is, but *something*."

The girl sniffed at the word *something*. Wayward girl that she was, she still thought she had a heritage and that she surpassed Jimmie.

Jimmie thought that if he had her alone for ten minutes, he'd teach her to sniff; though he did not consciously know what he meant by the thought, something less blunt but more compelling than a beating or sexual havoc.

"You want help with the meals, Mister cook?" he persisted.

"Ah, the practical turn of mind of the nomadic food-gatherer. We Europeans look on the primitive life as an idyllic if not poetic state of mind. But in fact the primitive life is beset with practical issues, and primitive man must have a mind to them."

The girl continued to look smug that the cook could beat people over the head with rhetoric.

"I ain't a primitive, Mister cook." It was Mr Neville whom Jimmie had first heard use the word, often with wan eyes and in groans.

The cook persisted in a silence, to make Jimmie feel foolish or state what in fact he was. What could he say?

"I'm a half-breed. My father's an important man in Brentwood."

Again Jimmie felt reason to hate the girl, her adenoidal disbelief.

"Oh yes, Jimmie?" the cook asked. "What was he in Brentwood?"

The wholesome image of Mr Neville entered Jimmie Blacksmith's mind. "He was a minister of religion."

"My God, you do use your indefinite articles well, Jimmie. I've never met a black who could even use one before."

"I don't know what those are, Mister cook. All I know is yer really want t' make me out a fool."

"Now, Jimmie, you know I didn't intend—"

"All I know, Mister cook, and I know it bloody well . . ." (He could feel a certain power of speech in him and knew his eyes were flashing.) ". . . all I know is I never leave a job until I finished it. Unless I was workin' for a evil man. A man from Merriwa district, a unjust man. And another evil man I left."

The girl was at first impressed by his appeal to the virtue of his labour. But the cook chuckled, as if Jimmie had missed the point, and then suggested that they'd be late with the lunches if they didn't start work immediately.

In furious heat, with a film of sweat on her upper lip, the girl went off across the yard to make superior food ready for Mr and Mrs Hayes.

Jimmie Blacksmith had Wellingtons he had bought in Cowra, where the lady in the shop had called them gumboots. Knowing the military suggestion in the name, Jimmie preferred to call them Wellingtons. He felt they defined his outline, and was correct; so that shearers began to say, "That Jimmie, he isn't like any other black I saw."

It was astonishing but the truth that whites looked on black feet in boots as a guarantee against the nomadic drive that had spoiled the working record of all black people.

Living up to the guarantee, Jimmie worked out the entire season with the one shearing contractor.

When the season ended, Jimmie swept up the floor on a station about forty miles from the Hayeses'. Only a fortnight before, Mrs Hayes and her wayward girl, Gilda, had come visiting the station-owner's wife. Once again, Jimmie had found the girl and the cook speaking deeply in the shearers' kitchen; but soon she had sought out Jimmie himself and explained herself. They had come then to an arrangement.

The arrangement grew from an accidental meeting with each other some months earlier, on the riverbank at Hayeses'. They had been together for a few hours then, had made love so dismal that Jimmie, at the summer's end when the arrangement was made, could scarcely remember a single tone of its emotion or even a physical feature of it.

But the arrangement had been made and now he had to collect his pay and act upon it.

So the floor was swept for the last time. A card-table was brought in from the homestead and the contractor sat at it and paid the men in banknotes.

Family men planned to take most of their pay home for winter in Cowra or Forbes or Orange. There were still the spree-happy, who put part of the bonus in their boots, so that they might arrive at the far-end of a week of dedicated excess with the price of a train fare home.

Money was counted and counted again with luxurious lack of haste and then folded intimately into pockets.

Two of the younger men were going to womanize and drink until they had nothing, and then go off to Sydney to join the Mounted Rifles. For the *Bulletin* and the cook had both kept them informed on the war in South Africa.

It was the beginning of southern autumn, 1900.

Jimmie was paid last. Amidst small conclaves plotting happiness, he and the contractor were ignored. In the joy and yelping, the contractor thought for a second and held out

£3 to Jimmie. Jimmie would not take it, but backed away.

"Fair go, boss," he said. "I'm gettin' married."

The man blew tobacco smoke with his bottom lip, up through his tarnished ginger moustache. He picked up three more notes.

"Ten bob a week, boss. Say yer will!"

"Yer fuckin' relatives only drink it."

"No, boss. I'm marryin'. White girl."

"What white girl?"

"Missus Hayes' girl, boss."

"Did yer git her in the family way?"

"What, boss?"

"Yer sow a piccaninny in her?"

"Yair. She's nice girl. Out of a home."

"I wouldn't boast about the white girl if I was you."

He snatched up two more notes, in token of the hopelessness of Jimmie's marriage with the nice girl out of a home, and as if he felt he must choose between paying some debt now rather than later.

"Bugger orf, Jimmie," he said. "While yore lucky."

The Hayeses' maid said she respected him. Helped to it, of course, because she carried his child. She was very young and her legs were freckled.

Yet Jimmie had seen in her a chance of white marriage very soon after their first meeting, or at least very soon after that Sabbath incident on the riverbank. Even then he had observed her. She was very stupid.

For example, Mrs Hayes had shown her—out of Mrs Beeton's illustrated book——how table should be set and how dinner should be served. Yet Gilda was all the time in a panic of forgetting it all. If you spied on the Hayeses' dining-room of an evening you would see Mrs Hayes's vigilance, Mr Hayes's resentment of not serving himself, and you could hear Gilda's hisses and snufflings as she scuttered about the room with tureens and salvers and the potatoes went cold. It was then that you understood her sniff conveyed no shred of superior pride. She had bad sinuses, and a terror of being sent back to the home for the wayward. Nor was she Mrs Healy. But a start had to be made somewhere with white women. And

50

Jimmie could not help thinking that under the pressure of his coming successes she might be converted into some sort of Mrs Healy.

Jimmie Blacksmith was to find them a domicile and then she was to leave the Hayeses' service and join him.

One month later he was settled with a fencing contract for a man called Newby who owned 7,000 acres near Wallah. He could cut wood from the Newbys' property and make a split-timber one-room home for his bride. He dug a cesspit.

The fifty-two-year-old farmer, leaning back in the privacy of his shovel-shaped beard and irony of his cold prominent eyes, seemed to spend a considerable time watching him. All the time he sucked a pebble to keep his mouth moist.

As if they had all conspired, Mr Newby—like Healy and Lewis—seemed to have made a sport out of waiting for Jimmie Blacksmith to behave in what he would have considered *character*.

To indicate that he might not, Jimmie Blacksmith would open up responsible subjects of conversation.

"Lookin' f'ward to federation, boss?"

"I'm not lookin' f'ward or back, Jimmie. Free trade won't hurt us farmers. The politicians can do what they want. They do anyhow. When's yer wife comin', Jimmie?"

"Soon. Don't yer think it'll make the country strong?"

Newby would laugh.

"What do yer care if the country's strong?"

"I'm a patriot, boss." Saying such things, Jimmie scarcely knew whom he was mocking: himself, Newby, Australia.

"Yer ought go into politics."

"D'yer reckon, Mr Newby?"

"I seen worse politicians than you, Jimmie. Old Taylor from Mudgee who got sent out of the House for pissing behind a pillar on the very floor of the parliament in Sydney. And the things they done to make sure the railways passed their door. Yer get a town like Walcha—thousands of people—does the train go there? No, it goes to a place where there's no town, fifteen miles away. Just so some bloody squatter in parliament don't have to haul his wool any distance to a railhead. They're scandalous, those blokes. Yer wouldn't be the biggest rascal among 'em, Jimmie. Yer reckon yer wife's white?"

"White 's white, boss. No blackie in her."

"What about the little blackie yer started in her? Eh, Jimmie, yer filthy bastard?"

"It happens more'n yer think, boss."

"Don' tell me what happens. I know what bloody happens."

Healy, Lewis, now Newby had each staked his soul on Jimmie's failure. If they were so supreme on their land that they didn't need to be political, why should they yearn so for Jimmie's mistakes; and, when mistakes were not made, dream them up? He had even begun remotely to wonder if a man's only means of treating with them was to "declare war". It was a phrase he had picked up on the shearing floor the previous year. It connoted for him a sweet wide freedom —to hate, discredit, debase as an equal.

But Newby was more immediately kindly than anyone else had been. He had three daughters, a wife, a female lodger. Perhaps all that had taught him concern for women.

"How's that fiancée of yours getting here, Jimmie?"

"Train to Lithgow, boss, then train to Gilgandra."

"But yer ain't goin' t' walk a potted lady all the way from Gilgandra to here?"

"I don' know what to do, Mr Newby."

"Better take my second girl's hack. Jest walk him. Yer kin come and git him when it's time. What way did yer say she was coming?"

Jimmie repeated the route, which tickled Newby—that a black should be able to remember itineraries.

"Bloody nice girl, boss," Jimmie found himself admitting one day. "Kin cook, kin serve at table. Very nice. Knows where a person's soup spoon ought t' be. Trained by a sheepman's wife. Mrs Hayes. From Cowra."

Mr Newby nodded. But there was always mockery in the corners of his eyes, on the remoter side of his face.

Wallah on the river was a straggle of fifteen houses wide apart. It had a telegraph relay-station, a police station, a pub, and two churches. The Methodist church and residence was on a hillock of its own, with its black and gold board announcing times of services. A name had recently been painted out on the board and *The Rev. T. S. Treloar B.A.* substituted there.

Before Jimmie had reached the residence gate, the parson appeared at the door in his shirtsleeves and stock, a hammer in his hand. The hammer reminded Jimmie of the Rev. Mr Neville's assiduity in the face of jerry-built manses.

With him was a large woman, hatted, who produced an echo of passion in him which he couldn't identify. Her face rose above arms full of lilies, roses and anenomes. The blue coat was evocative too.

Mrs Healy. Plenteous Mrs Healy. The evocation declined to become a sadness for himself and the neutral figure of Gilda Howie, the thin frightened girl-child he would marry.

He had always presumed that to marry a white raised a person in the community. Now it came to him that if one reject married another, the facts of their individual rejections might be added or even multiplied.

He suppressed this suspicion for fear of having to unmake his mind to marry, for fear too of Newby's mockery. To have a white wife and a good reputation for work—these must combine for a man's good.

The woman was flushed with sitting near the parson's fire, whose sweet white smoke scudded up the chimney.

"Very well, Mr Treloar. I won't hold you up. I'll go over to the vestry and arrange these."

"I don't think you quite understood what I said, Mrs Herne. I'd rather you didn't deck the church out with flowers."

"But I always . . . I mean, when we lived in Gunning . . ."

"There is more room for the Divine in an unadorned church. That's what I feel. However, if you wanted to give them to Mrs Treloar they'd be very welcome about the house."

"I picked them for . . . I mean, Mister Grant in Gunning used to . . ."

"But you see, this is my responsibility. It would be very much against my conscience if I were to introduce changes that weren't in the spirit of Methodism. I don't want to deny your kindness but . . ."

The woman's full cheeks had gone a very lusty pink.

"And *I* don't want to leave less room for the Divine in your house or in your church. I wished I'd remained Anglican. They are, at least, polite."

"Now I've offended you."

"Would you say so? Good afternoon, Mr Treloar."

Away she went towards the pub where, no doubt, her husband and dray were waiting. Jimmie sidled in through the garden gate she had left wide open.

At close range, the parson was very young with soft wet lips. A square-jawed young woman came out of the house and found him abstracted, mouth bunched in pain.

"Is she gone?"

"Yes."

"Why don't you just speak up to these rotten sows? You soon speak up to me. You're bloody-well not backwards in that."

"Ssh!" said the parson, still gazing at the garden path, the pruned stubs of rose-bushes. "Please, dearest, you mustn't say those things. Not in that way."

"Bloody mealy-mouth, that's you."

"Please, Enid, it's little use calling me names."

Already Mrs Treloar had spotted taut Jimmie Blacksmith waiting on the pathway.

"We don't want any wood cut, thank you," she called.

"It isn't wood, missus. I want t' git married."

"Today?"

"Saturdee week, missus."

"I suppose you know the normal stipend is a guinea."

"Enid!"

"Well, he can't expect to get married for nothing."

"Kin I pay yer today?"

"By all means." The parson shrugged his sadness off. "Of course."

After seeing the guinea into her husband's hand and pocket, Mrs Treloar moved back into her house. Her shoulders were held broad in an over-masculine way. She was tense with hatred, as others had been. It baffled Jimmie, with his simple hopes, that they should all be such dedicated haters.

"You had just better give me the details," said the parson. "Who is your intended? I mean, what is her name? If she

54

comes from a reserve we have to seek the permission of the superintendent."

Jimmie told him she was not from a station. She was white.

"No tarbrush," he said, for private vengeance; for the whites had something of a tribal mentality too, in that they hated to hear that one of their girls was going to a darkie. Even nice whites, like Mr Treloar, might betray regret.

"Mr Blacksmith," said the minister, "Mr Blacksmith, have you considered the problems that might result? We must be practical about them. It is very possible that you could be much insulted."

The minister's politeness angered Jimmie. Quite brutally he said, "She got child, boss. From me she got a child. She wants t' git married in church, proper Methodist marriage."

The fact of her pregnancy routed Mr Treloar, and he asked Jimmie indoors. He put some wood on the fire and gave himself a splinter. There were some dead embers over the varnished floor and black velvet cushions on the settee. More remarkably still, there was a copy of the *Methodist Church Times* with vacant livings ringed in pencil. It could have been the Nevilles' front parlour.

"Can your future wife or yourself produce witnesses? Perhaps I should myself. They must be sober and so must you. No drink, you understand? My wife could be one of the witnesses," the man suggested with a grunt of pain. "And perhaps one of the wardens."

Jimmie was ready to go when Mrs Treloar came in in her militant manner. He could see Mr Treloar's eyes flinch.

"I do have some work for you to do," she said to Jimmie. "Please follow me."

"I'll cut any logs, Enid," offered the parson.

"You must keep out of it, please Theo."

Mr Treloar remaining with his plaintive eyes indoors; his spouse led Jimmie to a terrible heap of redwood, all tumbled blue and brown across Jimmie's track in the late light.

"You set to work please. I want it all cut and stacked."

"But missus, it's a ton an' a half."

"It's two tons. It will do your soul good. If you stop I'm fetching the police."

Seated on the wooden steps, her grey frock drooping between her boyishly held knees, she saw him to work. Four hours it took.

In half that time his hands were itching with sweat. He would stop to blow on them. It was madness, but still Mr Treloar was not to be seen. He must have been indoors with his purple pencil and his *Church Times*. Jimmie stacked the wood against the shed wall. Some badly knotted wood she permitted him not to cut.

Then he was allowed to drink water from the tank; there was a pannikin which he rinsed with care, just to show what a well-mannered boy he was.

He was more frightened than angry, not knowing what the lady was about. Dismissing him, she said, without a tremor of irony in the mouth or eyes, "Now you go home and pray every night."

He said he would.

So after thirteen nights of prayer, Jimmie was up before dawn and led one of the Newby hacks off towards Gilgandra.

Newby had flung an arm around the horse's neck, detaining it. "It's just for carrying yer missus, Jimmie. Yer kin lead him into Gilgandra, not ride him. Yer not the expectant mother. And Jimmie, they git sick, women I mean, all that weight on their tummy. So take it easy coming back."

Such terse kindnesses, even though kept within the limits of account-keeping, rose without warning from within Mr Newby. Had there been time for it Jimmie Blacksmith might have become his friend. As well, Jimmie could sense—but was too young to envy—a ferocious family love in the man, an impermeable knot of family love twelve miles east of Gilgandra.

So, faithfully, as if the beast were fitted with tachometer, Jimmie led and did not ride the hack into Gilgandra. At first he felt elated—intense winter sun and the dry cold flickering at his face.

About ten he could see through the heart of the town to the railhead and began to resent the insipid girl he had come to meet. He couldn't imagine how he would speak to her, what words he could use. Yet he faced a life-time of speaking to her.

The Express, belling like a church, rousing everyone's

chickens and maddening the hack, thrust its punitive cow-catcher at Jimmie in Gilgandra and stood still. The girl stepped down from the second-class observation deck. An old farmer from somewhat further west handed her luggage down and called, "Good luck, Mrs Blacksmith."

Unexpectedly, she clung to Jimmie so openly that he could see the old man's eyebrows at work behind the window. Did she perhaps love him, or did she need to convince herself she loved him, or did she believe that if she did all the things girls do in romances that she would be endowed with love?

The cruel thing was, as the farmer might have told her, that girls in romances don't allow themselves to be rolled by half-castes on a riverbank in the world's south.

"Darling," she said.

A pregnant woman could, as Newby predicted, be very uncomfortable on a horse, whether front-on or side-saddle; but after a mile or so, Gilda opted for side-saddle, and the bag, which Jimmie had up to now carried out of respect for Mr Newby's horseflesh, was then lashed to the pommel on the right side.

She seemed so young, so hopelessly twelve or thirteen, that he didn't look at her for fear of finding this afternoon's wedding, this evening's ritual of bedding, too blatantly crazy. So she sat, one leg cocked up high and sideways in a stirrup, clinging to pommel and cantle and snorting whenever she thought she was falling, snorting like an old man.

They made conversation.

"What was the train like?"

"Orright, Jimmie. It was cold in Lithgow. I thought I'd freeze."

"They reckon Lithgow's a bloody cold place."

"How's the new job goin', Jimmie?"

"It's orright. Boss is better than some others I know. It's a big job, should keep me goin' rest of the year."

"That's good. Is the minister orright?"

"The minister's orright. He got a bloody tartar for a wife."

"How d'yer mean?"

"Made me chop up whoppin' load of timber. For nothin'."

"The hide of her!"

"She was jealous. She ain't happy with the minister."

They laughed. It was their first married dialogue.

The witnesses were Mrs Treloar and the promised warden. The lady kept both eyebrows raised throughout, sceptical of the value of the Methodist form of marriage *vis-à-vis* the Blacksmiths. The warden was a sour old Wesleyan with rugged brows and a jaw like a peninsula. But he caused no trouble.

After the rite, Mrs Treloar called Gilda aside for a long talk by the vestry door.

At the gate, Mr Treloar went from foot to foot, aching for the right words.

"Well, Jimmie, a big day, eh? A very important day. I hope you're very happy, you and Mrs Blacksmith. The Newbys, I'm sure, will be very kind."

Mrs Treloar kept on, persuading Gilda of something. Mr Treloar was coughing and, trapped by the paucity of gestures, found himself offering Jimmie his hand far too early.

"Yes," he said, reddening, "the Newbys will be very kind. I often have the family to services here and you must feel welcome to . . . come if you want."

"I ain't got no proper clo'es," Jimmie told him, "No suit or nothin'."

"Well . . . I'm sure a good worker like you soon will have."

Meanwhile, Mrs Treloar had intense hold of Gilda's arm, giving counsel that could possibly be worth the guinea.

Mr Treloar called jollily: "I'm going in now, love." As if she were open to hints.

Ten minutes later, Gilda was dismissed and joined her husband. Again they had the use of the hack.

Now Gilda Blacksmith and Jimmie had their second marital dialogue.

"What was Mrs Treloar beltin' yer ear about?"

"Stuff I didn't think any parson's wife'd know."

"What sort of stuff?"

"How to avoid having babies."

"None of her affair."

"That's what I thought. But yer can't say nothin'."

It came to Jimmie that although they were church-wed and had been named a family, they still had very little right of reply in a population that sprouted blunt precept.

58

"Some of the stuff I couldn't tell yer. It was . . . well, she couldn't have learned it from Mr Treloar."

"If anyone's learnin' anythin', it'd proberly be that poor bastard."

All over the pastures of the rich farmers of Wallah, a melancholy wash of deep green let you know that night was coming and you had not yet reached home.

The girl changed in mood, and began to cry secretively when they sighted the little one-room house with its flue of beaten tin. The floor was earth and cold. There was a hessian bag inside the door as a doormat.

They lay on the bed, for the journey had drained them. It was a mercy that neither was in the mood for loveplay, for suddenly they felt defeated, two conspirators trying to get into that other ether where the Hayeses and Newbys subsisted, trying in bafflement to learn the rites, the motives and notions.

Gilda, in fact, wanted to die. For weeks she had told herself that she would have a new house. These ideas become aggrandized in the tight secret minds of girls who come from houses of charity to shovel potatoes onto Mrs Hayes's plate. Now Gilda found herself in a definite one-room shack, she wept . . . although she had known that this was all she could expect; and if Jimmie had asked her what else she wanted she could not have answered. She knew well enough what her rights were. She could feel them in her marrow. They were not ample rights.

As night came on, Jimmie found himself making white promises about the land they would come to own and the people who would call them *sir* or *madam*. He was desperate to soothe this girl he did not love, without knowing why he tried. Perhaps he did not want to be caught by the momentum of her despair, which became more explicit the more she wept.

A slowly descending white was wedded to a black in the ascendant. That was what Jimmie hoped had happened. He hoped they might survive on his momentum.

"Jimmie's a nigger," he said, "an' he'll work like a bloody nigger."

Afterwards, in the bright night, she made him some corned

beef and potatoes. That made her feel better. An exercise of domesticity.

Mrs Newby, a durable lady with mannishly jutted jaw, visited the new home and told Gilda to make a list of household necessaries, which she herself would buy in town on Friday and bring home in the dray.

Then she questioned Gilda about her pregnancy, whether her ankles had swollen, were her veins playing up. All the time she twitched at the small clutch of hairs that grew from a mole on the underside of her jaw. She gave advice out of her own wide practice of child-bearing.

"If he beats yer or hurts yer," she said, "yer kin come straight to me."

"I don't think he'll do anything like that."

"Also, yer kin have yer little one at my place. We've got a big range and lots of linen."

For this invitation to an away birth, Gilda was grateful. If by an outside chance (and there were outside chances) the child was clearly someone else's, Jimmie could not make too much fuss in the formidable Newby household; and would become reconciled.

She was sure Jimmie had a talent for becoming reconciled, for he was gentle and tentative with her. She did not know it was for fear of loving or having pity for her. To a woman he loved he would have been far more intense and far less gentle.

The weather grew colder. Jimmie worked passionately. Gilda played at wifeliness by bringing him his lunch along the boundary fence each day and by calling him *dearest*. It was his hope that they would both soon get over this coy segment of their marriage.

Every Friday, Gilda took her constantly rehearsed, arduously copper-plated grocery list to Newbys'. On Saturdays she went to make the collection. Thus she came to identify the monoliths of the Newby household. There was Mrs Newby, her own monument to motherhood, though small farts or belches could be expected to emit from such structural grandeur without apology at the apex of uplifting talk.

The home paragon was Miss Petra Graf, schoolmistress at Wallah, lodger at the Newbys'. Against her the Newby girls, who were big, meaty, thick-pored, could try their opinions and discover how viable they might be in proper company. For although Miss Graf was a big country girl herself and could eat a pound of steak without feeling satiated, she gave off a soft musk of delicacy and knew etiquette.

These four sounded and resounded about the Newby kitchen, especially on Saturday mornings, when Miss Graf was at the end of her week's work. There was a younger sister of four and a brother of eleven.

Mr Newby and both his big boys were hard workers and one rarely saw them at home. On Saturday the boys played Rugby and raised what Cain they could in Gilgandra.

So that there was an ascetic femininity about the Newby homestead that disturbed Gilda. There was the acrid warmth of mother Newby and the distant virginity of Miss Graf.

Besides being finer in texture than the Newby girls, Miss Graf also had it over them in that she was engaged to a squatter's son in Gulargambone, where her German grandparents sat out the inverted seasons with astounding, almost irrelevant (since they were in their nineties) grimness of purpose.

The Newby women all mimed Petra Graf's low-keyed horror at Gilda's situation. They even took her to church in a punitive sort of way and hustled exactly marked hymnbooks into her hands.

Contact on the level of Mr Newby and Jimmie Blacksmith continued blunt.

"How yer goin' to raise yer piccaninny, Jimmie?"

"He be no piccaninny, boss. He three parts white."

"Yair. And his kid'll be an eighth black and his a sixteenth. But it doesn't matter how many times yer descendants bed down, they'll never get anything that don't have the tarbrush in it. And it'll always spoil 'em, that little bit of somethink else."

In his way, Newby could be hard to be angry with, for he spoke as if condoling Jimmie for a sad disease which did not reflect on the patient, even though it implied fatal blindness in Jimmie's sense of what society allowed.

But Jimmie had worked so well that Newby now owed him fifteen pounds. Occasionally the farmer strolled over to insult him in the hope that he would stalk off without payment. This was common rural practice and whenever it failed, Newby would at least show Jimmie a sort of knockabout respect and call him a cunning black sod. Now and then, looking up from the wedges, Jimmie would see one or both of the Newby boys superbly mounted, depicted in long crystals of light through the prismatic sweat of his eyebrows. Even then he was thinking that a man could not go on for ever playing the willing nigger.

When Gilda's time was near, Mrs Newby and Miss Graf and both the elder Misses Newby took Gilda away to the homestead. With terrible zeal they set about the management of her parturition. They waited out her fear and contractions and told her that the pain would help her to love her child all the better. The Newby sisters knotted their chins against her screams; hadn't she earned them?

The birth was quite normal, and the Newby girls learned a great deal. Jimmie was not allowed to see the child for several hours—he was kept squatting by the woodheap. One at a time the Newby men rode in from their work and were permitted into the house. They could be heard clomping around the kitchen and came onto the veranda to call out such things as:

"Congratulations, Jimmie. I believe yer have a real genuine white."

The lamps had been lit when Mrs Newby came out to call Jimmie.

"I want to show yer yer son. Will yer behave yerself, Jimmie?"

"Christ, missus, I ain't a savage."

"Orright. Come on."

They went through the wide high kitchen, large as a Methodist chapel, and through into the sitting-room. Here a fire burnt and gave the green velvet furniture—the best out of the catalogue—a cosy sheen. Gilda was not about. Miss Graf stood in front of the fire, a baby in her arms.

"Mr Blacksmith," said Miss Graf, "I should like to show you the boy-child your wife has given birth to."

The baby's blankets were formed like a capuche above its wizened head, but now Miss Graf pulled them back. The querulous, bubbling face writhed slightly and Jimmie took a survey of the features.

It was not his child. He could tell, though not with reasons, that he could not have begotten a child of that face. He wished he had, his hand was already out towards the child, an arrested movement of fatherliness. He thought how close he must have been to siring it; the cruel odds of the seed.

At a second look, he could tell immediately whose child it was. The superior cook's. But *he* would never have married Gilda. A dense girl like that would interfere with one's study of Fabian socialism.

"What do yer think of him, Mr Blacksmith?" Mrs Newby asked as meaningfully as anyone could.

"Orright. Yer kin all laugh now. He ain't my baby."

"You can't be sure," said Miss Graf. "Certainly, it doesn't look as if . . . Anyhow, I don't think it'd be wise for you to see your wife tonight."

"I must say," Mrs Newby said, bowing to her own necessities, and twiddling her hairy mole, "that I think her conduct is dreadful and I sympathize with you, Mr Blacksmith."

Jimmie stood aching for some sacramental word to be said that might alter the nature of the bundle so that it became his. He felt certain that there was something that could be amended easily, coitus being such a random thing.

Coitus is random. Children are definite. This child was definitely the cook's. What Jimmie could nearly have begged for aloud was to have it re-consigned to its origins and arrangements made at the source so that it should show up in Miss Graf's arms as his.

Miss Graf was speaking to him. Her light brown hair was brought forward onto the top of her head and her neck seemed white marble in the fire-light.

"Will you be angry with her, Mr Blacksmith?"

Jimmie snorted. Knowing he would not touch Gilda; he would despise and leave her body unmarked.

He said, "I had a right t' think it was my kid."

"Indeed you did. I want you to promise me here that you'll never strike her for this."

Enchanted by the statuesque girl he nodded three times. Then she said, "You should let her go now. And the baby.

63

There's others better set up to look after them."

But he said nothing. His blood drummed. Miss Graf did not move, nor doubt that she was the one appointed to say whether he was finished with the persons of his marriage. The blood in his ears sizzled.

"No, you fat bitch!" he called out in the secrecy of his belly.

On his way home, the Newby boys made a few bird sounds and asked him if he'd seen any cuckoos about.

He didn't understand what they were talking about.

Of course, Gilda told him over and over that she had been certain it was his, that it was astounding to her that the baby should have the cook's long head.

There was high moral glee in the women of the homestead. There was uncouthness on the veranda where old Newby chortled and doubled that Jimmie should have been shotgunned into the wedding.

Jimmie Blacksmith was bereft, but there was not enough to Gilda to warrant sustained hatred. She had a wispiness of soul. The marriage, to exist, needed a child. His child, not the cook's long-domed child.

"It's a trick many a boy's had tried out on him," Newby told Jimmie Blacksmith. "*Marry me because I'm pregnant.* Sometimes she's not pregnant at all. Sometimes she is by someone else. Her husband has his doubts all his life. But yer don't have any doubts. There isn't a grain of native in him. He looks like a Supreme Court Judge."

7

FIVE DAYS LATER, Tabidgi Jack Smolders arrived with Jimmie's initiation tooth. With him were laughing Mort and a boy called Peter, a cousin. Sauntering up the road from Wallah, they surprised Jimmie at his work.

When they saw Jimmie's surprise, Tabidgi began to chant high up in his nose, a runic circular chant. Mort danced, laughing, miming some long-necked beast spying into a haven to see if brother or enemy were there.

"Come fer booze?" Jimmie asked them. "I ain't got no booze."

He hoped they had come for mean reasons. For he felt guilty before the unbudging wrinkles of Tabidgi's face.

Jackie Smolders took the white tooth from his left, cleaner, unmagicked pocket and offered it to Jimmie with cupped hands.

"Yer got married t' white girl. Tooth'll keep yer safe."

"It'll keep me safe, will it?"

Jimmie struck Tabidgi's hands apart. The admonitory and guardian tooth flew into long grass. Everyone was silent, the fourteen-year-old appalled. Mort took him by the shoulder and began to hunt in the grass.

Jimmie was thinking what idiot bastards they were to approach him with such high tribal seriousness.

But, finding the tooth, Mort held it up and he and Peter

65

knelt in the grass and beamed. So that Jimmie Blacksmith was suddenly ashamed and overcome with a fatalism native to his blood, the fatalism that had kept him at Verona once against his will.

Now he understood that Jackie Smolders would stay and, very likely, drink what he could. And Mr Newby would call more frequently and drop blunt hints.

But the tooth would still have been brought if there had been no such thing as fermented liquor or Mr Newby's attitudes. For the tooth gave tribal safeguards against the unknown sortilege of a white woman's body.

Jimmie Blacksmith received it, excised with stone in his thirteenth year, and stuffed it into his pocket.

"Orright. It's good o' yer t' go t' the trouble. It's a long walk yer come."

In invocatory style, Tabidgi recited all the well-omened places they had passed, all the evil grounds too, to find their kinsman in his need. Tabidgi's utterance in these matters verged on the holy, the lore in his drunken old head made of it a holy stone. He could not be sent away like that, as if fermented liquour were the whole truth of him.

So Tabidgi, Mort and Peter—but particularly Mort—constructed a lean-to by the Blacksmiths' place. Gilda could not refuse that, having the cook's child to explain away, having Jimmie to palliate.

With his uncle and giggling Mort and the boy Peter, he did not mention the cook, for pride's sake. Perhaps they never knew and if they had known would not have considered it significant.

It surprised him that he was apologetic towards his kin who had brought back to him, almost physically with the tooth, the incisive canons of tribal kinship.

"Tell Tabidgi to bugger off back to Brentwood," Jimmie instructed Mort but would not do it himself.

He consoled himself by beating Gilda a few times. Once he beat her because he found a cut-out advertisement for a Twin-Vulcan kitchen range. The nullity of her ambition to possess one mocked his own soured dreams. His fist flew for the little hollow beneath her temple. She did not know why she was being beaten, but seemed to think it was one of the normal exchanges between married people. He could spend a long time looking down at the child and Gilda would stand passive and withdrawn but ready to protect her child's flesh.

Jimmie would stand by the baby and covet it. When discovered, he would walk away.

"Grow up t' be fuckin' white know-all. Won't want t' know me when he grow up."

A very frail, thin-hipped girl, Gilda had grown sickly since the birth. Her heels were so reduced and sharp that she was always sewing away at holes they made in stockings, strange, punched holes, not the holes of ordinary wear.

Her child made her welcome. No one else did, though moon-eyed Peter was often willing to sit by the cradle of the white child with its little down-turned white nose.

Not knowing he was an elder and that the runes of antiquity were written in his boozy old mind, she feared and hated Jackie Smolders.

At the homestead the big, meaty, moral women considered her triply fallen, for piling black marriage on white conception on black fornication. Miss Graf told her there were homes for unfortunate women, that they didn't have to cleave to a black.

It was not hard for Miss Graf to suppose that society guaranteed its members against certain ultimate shames. That was what charity was about.

Miss Graf transmitted such presumptions to the Newby girls; so that Mrs Newby could say at Friday shopping in Gilgandra, "It's been so good for the girls to have Miss Graf staying at the homestead. She's got real tone."

Every morning Jimmie hoped for Tabidgi's departure. He considered putting bad omens on the bagging where Jackie Smolders slept—a butchered barn owl, strange stones, rags dipped in blood which Tabidgi might presume to be menstrual and so fatally potent. But these were always projects for tomorrow, recourses almost as final as beating him away with branches.

And because the child in the house was not his and showed up the folly of his white marriage, he somehow felt unequal to making a strong expulsion of his maternal uncle.

Now he worked automatically, without aim. Work was a sedative for a man with a magic uncle bent on liquor, a lying wife, a bastard child; all within his walls.

Mort helped Jimmie work. Not wanting any definite return for it.

Certainly Mort had matured. Sometimes, however, he would snigger at bulge-eyed, shovel-bearded Newby sucking at his pebble. When he hit his knuckle with a mallet one day he crowed with laughter as long as the pain endured.

Their work was not an economic success. Two divided the labour but did not double the work rate. Most of his day Jimmie spent in a private frenzy, as if seeking space of his own amongst all the strangers who had claim on him. To mock Tabidgi's laziness he might hunt possums at night, perhaps for half the night. So there was always the soft meat of phalangers for Jack Smolders and thin Gilda (who got very sick of it).

Easily, without his noticing it, the possum-hunting became for him something more than a duty of hospitality. It was an inverted sort of testing of God, Gilda, the Newbys, his tribe. It was only when he had given all the justice that was in him, rendered what he could to each, that he would be entitled to stand back and declare himself accursed. And knowing himself such, he would have untold liberties of rage and rampage.

Every night he would buffet and rut away against Gilda, threatening that she'd bear a blackie yet. Her menstrual blood put him to flight one night. It was the very taboo he had thought of using against Jackie. Patronizingly, he had thought that an old savage like Jackie would be flummoxed by it.

Now, flummoxed himself, he climbed into the lean-to and lay down near Mort, shivering and hating God.

Late on a Friday morning, in the frosts of July, Mrs Gilda Blacksmith went to the homestead to leave her weekly order. She did not take her baby with her.

Coming to the home-yard gate she could see, in the sun in the angle of the two-winged house, Mr Newby napping in an upholstered chair. He was dressed for town in a butterfly collar and tweed suit.

Sitting on the veranda boards, also dressed for town, were the two sons. Both had their coats open, showing off the slim strength their vests defined. One had a homburg tipped over his eyes. All night they had worked bagging wheat at the old homestead (now used for silage) a mile away. They planned to work the whole of the Friday night as well.

She stood still, remembering the day Mr Newby had come across her and her baby by accident. He had been droving steers to new pasture. Gilda always avoided him if she could, but he rolled up to her on his horse, vaulted out of the saddle and exposed his patriarchal blunt genitals, slug-white and sitting in his hand for her information.

"When yer find a bigger'n than that on a nigger, Mrs Blacksmith, let me know."

Within ten seconds he was covered and back in the saddle. His dogs were barking and the sullen cattle moved.

Now, on the Friday, she hoped to creep past his dozing form. But as she put her foot on the bottom step, Mr Newby woke.

"G'day, Mrs Blacksmith. Kin I do somethink?"

"I jest wanted to give in me order."

He stared sympathetically at her crushed dress of green muslin. Freckles and poor pearls of sweat were on her cheeks.

"But I'm sorry," he told her. "I spoke to yer husband. I told him I couldn't go on f'warding him advances in the form of groceries. Not since the place has turned into a blacks' camp like that. I'm never certain whether he'll git any work done next week or not. I don't want to be left with an unfinished boundary. I made that clear to yer husband, Mrs Blacksmith. The cure's in his hands."

His half-drowsy edict made her want to assent and get clean away. At least the baby has my milk, she thought.

"Sorry, Mr Newby." She began backing.

"No. Yer looked knocked up. Make yerself a cup of tea in the kitchen there. No one'll disturb yer. I'm jest waiting on the women. Oh, yer better knock, though. Miss Graf's home for the day with influenza."

Gilda noticed that one of his cunning sons snickered with closed eyes at the mention of Miss Graf and her influenza.

In fact, she found Miss Graf in the kitchen, in a flannel

nightgown pulled tight about her neck; breathing bronchiti-
cally and occasionally pushing a small handkerchief to the tip
of her nose. Gilda stared, as she was meant to, at the un-
attainable degree of womanhood Miss Graf achieved even in
the deeps of winter influenza.

Yet what had that boy been chortling for?

"Come in, Mrs Blacksmith."

"Mr Newby told me to git meself a cuppa tea."

"By all means. I wonder would you care to make one for
me? Tea's on the mantel."

"Yair, miss."

She busied about to distract the schoolmistress from making
her onerous judgments.

"How's your baby?"

"Well, Miss Graf."

"Have you left him at home?"

"Yairs, Miss Graf. With Peter."

"Peter?"

"The boy, Miss Graf."

"The black boy?"

"Yairs, Miss Graf."

"Well, I mustn't keep you too long."

"Orright, Miss Graf."

Gilda spotted rosary beads around Miss Graf's neck,
tucked away into her bosom. In the home for wayward girls,
the chaplain had impressed on the wayward girls that Papists
were dense, unwashed and subject to secret witchcraft. Poor
remnants on the margin of the progress of man. How unfair
then that Miss Graf should seem to be centre stage, to *own*
the book of moral judgment.

Her pedagogy was said to be severe, and the farmers of
Wallah approved of it.

A minute later Mrs Newby came from some deep part of
the house into the kitchen. Her dugs were ponderous as law
within her brown velvet.

"Mrs Blacksmith! I didn't expect ter see yer here this week.
Mr Newby told me yer wouldn't be ordering."

"Jimmie must've forgot to tell me, Mrs Newby."

"Mrs Blacksmith is kindly making us tea. Would you care
for a cup in your own house, Mrs Newby?"

"No time, dear. How's the baby boy, Mrs Blacksmith?"

"Very good, thank you."

Mrs Newby stared without too much apparent pity at the arduous bun Gilda had made of her back hairs.

"Yer hair looks nice, dear."

"Thank you, Mrs Newby."

"The baby's been left with the boy," said Miss Graf, as if this should qualify Mrs Newby's praise.

"What boy?"

"The aborigine boy Peter," Gilda pleaded. "He's got so heavy, you know. The baby."

Mrs Newby advanced one massive button-up boot.

"Is the boy trustworthy?"

"He's a nice boy, Peter," Gilda pleaded.

"It's yore child, Mrs Blacksmith. But a white baby oughtn't let be grow up with tribal blacks."

"Peter likes him. Peter's very gentle."

"Did you know I was getting married in the new year?" Miss Graf asked.

"Congratulations, miss," Gilda told her, as if a merely and mildly social reason were behind Miss Graf's news.

"What I wanted to say was that I'm sure we, my future husband and I, could employ you at *Wallabadah*. That's the name of my fiancé's property."

"It's yer chance!" Mrs Newby whispered. "Yer'll only lose that child of yores if yer stay with the blacks."

The four-year-old, Mrs Newby's late fruit, came in and looked at her conspiring mother with green eyes, the family's best. If I had a child as safe as you are safe, Gilda thought.

"You'd have your own room, Mrs Blacksmith, and be able to have the baby with you all the time."

But Gilda was no simpleton. She knew with some exactness how long an employer like Miss Graf could tolerate her. When the soup was cold, the saucepans boiled dry, the wedding silver tarnished, the bone china cracked, Miss Graf would with regret cast Mrs Blacksmith and her bastard back on the public care.

Both the elder Newby girls came in in velvet and Gilda had to explain again what had happened to her child—that he was in the care of a savage.

71

According to the Sydney *Mail*, said one of the Newby girls, blacks *ate* each other in Queensland.

To Gilda came the image of the pensive ages the boy Peter spent contemplating the deal box her baby lay in; endlessly willing to pluck the child's rattle and hear its belly-rumbles of satisfaction.

"I'm Christian-married to Jimmie," she pleaded.

"They're not Christian. It doesn't matter what yer are—Methodist, Catholic. But not all the missionaries in the British Empire ever turned one black into a Christian. Are there any black bishops?" Mrs Newby knew well enough there weren't. It would have been in the Sydney *Mail* if there were. "Are there even any black ministers of religion?"

"The Benedictine priests," said Miss Graf, "did—I believe—ordain three aboriginal priests."

"And what happened?" all the Newbys wanted to know.

"They all wandered off. Not one of the three was seen again."

"I think Miss Graf's made yer a Christian offer," Mrs Newby decreed.

"Thank you, Miss Graf."

"Thanks won't get yer far. Yer force me to say it. Yore a scandal t' all of us."

The women watched Gilda avidly, as if waiting for her to take some decision owed to them. Why was she depended on? Why did large, tough women pretend she threatened them? What was it that excommunicated her? For she was humble and would have accepted any morsel of grace they might extend her.

Suddenly she heard, as if from another person's throat, creaking noises of bemusement in her own mouth. That sneering Newby boy had had Miss Graf, Gilda wanted to say; and how was it *they* could evade being encircled and judged?

On the range the kettle sang. No one took notice of it. Meanwhile the elder Newby girl gratuitously pledged on the spot that she would never marry any black.

Mrs Newby's long belly growled. "Yer grieve us, miss. Yer must leave them natives."

"I beg you," said snuffling Miss Graf, "that you'll see the sense of my offer."

For no more than a second Miss Graf's authoritarian vowels carried to Gilda the pod-bursting smell of imprisoned spring in the yard where wayward girls were exercised. Gilda opened her mouth and began to roar in full voice. The four grown women and the child stared at her in her cold latitude of culpability.

"Aw, swallow it!" awakened Mr Newby called from his armchair on the veranda.

Gilda could not understand why it was that if she spoke of the day the patriarch had shown off his phallus it would shame *her* and no one else. She could not understand why she had no standing in the moral market-place.

When she ran out of the house, "Kin we drop yer part of the way, Mrs Blacksmith?" Mr Newby called.

His sons uttered thick laughter, as if they knew of their father's eccentricity towards her.

She did not stop sprinting until the homestead was lost somewhere behind her in the timber.

8

IN THE Blacksmith larder were a few pounds of flour, less than a pound of corned beef, one skinned possum, a portion of rice. There was also a quarter of a bottle of port—if such things counted—fetched full by Jackie Smolders from the pub in Wallah that Friday morning, along with a second one which Jackie and Mort had already drunk between them.

When Jimmie Blacksmith came into his house at dusk, the baby was crying and Gilda was sitting on the mattress, her legs awry like those of a flung doll. Her face was puckered with weeping in that corner cold as a cave.

She told him what Miss Graf wanted and that there were no groceries. Newby intended to starve him off (Jimmie could see), or was perhaps even ratifying Miss Graf's plan to pester the marriage, as poor a union as it was, apart.

First, Jimmie Blacksmith called on Jackie Smolders. Perhaps not merely because Mort was asleep: in his anger Jimmie may have returned to the Tullam instinct for primacy of mother's brother. Certainly he did not know his reasons himself.

For it was against all reason to take Tabidgi with him on a mission of complaint. Tabidgi was Newby's pretext for withholding supplies. Yet, at the other pole from tribal instincts, Jimmie may simply have wanted to demonstrate Jackie to the

74

Newbys, show them what a harmless old bugger he was.

Anyhow, Tabidgi was the one he took with him. The old man seemed a little flattered.

Jimmie Blacksmith went armed with his Enfield, though he did not intend it as his means of persuasion. In the sharp bright night he might bag something, possum or wallaby; or if the Newbys were obdurate, one of their cattle. He ranted, threats of more pervasive vengeance than that. "I'll derail a bloody train," he told Tabidgi. Derailing a train was the ultimate reprisal.

Tabidgi suggested a magical revenge. If Jimmie were to take *the* tooth and punch it into the track-marks of Newby's beasts, women, sons, in Newby's tracks themselves, nothing of Newby's would ever be able to walk straight again.

"Horseshit," said Jimmie Blacksmith.

His eye was on the distant radiance of the Newby kitchen. No old man's witchery with teeth and tracks for him. No waiting for Newby to feel the bite. Newby must feel the bite tonight.

When she opened the door, Mrs Newby herself was carrying a rifle slung loosely between armpit and elbow. Perhaps it was a habit from a harsh upbringing in wilder country than Wallah; perhaps she had been raised in the murderous lands around Charters Towers and had it drummed into her that one never answered the door without carrying arms. In any case it was only a formality. Now, although she could see Jimmie's Enfield, she dropped her own weapon in the corner by the door.

She was in her slippers and a comfortable dress, and was not easily made afraid.

"Possuming, Mr Blacksmith?" she suggested.

"Kin I see Mr Newby, missus? I want t' talk t' him about the groceries."

But Mr Newby was bagging wheat in the old farmhouse, she explained. The men would work there until the bagging was finished, because both the boys wanted to play Rugby in Gilgandra the next day.

They argued the point. Mrs Newby said her husband wasn't a charitable institution or somethink.

While they spoke, Jimmie caught sight of robust Miss Graf

indoors. Inappropriately to the debate he thought of how he had never had a girl like that, a plump, ripe girl. The black girls of the camps had ugly fat or tubercular leanness.

". . . so that I'm sure," Mrs Newby was saying, "if yer worked well enough and got rid of those hangers-on me husband'd be only too pleased to . . ."

"He owes me, missus. Nine hundred yards."

"I'm sure yer'll forgive me for believing me own husband."

As she began to close the door on him, he saw that Miss Graf was actually eaves-dropping intently, handkerchief rammed to her nose to hush the very rasp of her influenza, holding her breath with a plotter's rapacity for the appropriate facts.

Then in a second, Tabidgi and Jimmie Blacksmith were in the dark again and feeling very foolish.

"Wait 'n see the ole bugger in the morning," Tabidgi suggested.

But Jimmie felt close to a mandate to heap coals of fire on Newby's head. Newby must be tested tonight. Jimmie would not wait till morning without knowing if, in view of the cruelties he had suffered from Healy, Lewis, Farrell, Newby, the shearers' cook, he had a licence to run mad.

As they moved amongst the humble shapes of Newby's livestock, it seemed to Jimmie as if the question of their ownership had come up for decision. Tabidgi complained of rheumatism. Unendowed with the same sense of noblesse as Jimmie, he could see no sense in this second appeal to the Newbys.

The hurricane lights of Newby's old home showed up through the vacant windows. From fifty yards away, Jimmie could see one of the Newby boys working in an old satin-backed vest. There was a grating of shovels. Sweat was an art the Newbys knew. Others knew it too, from Mackay to Adelaide. From Eden to Tibooburra. Sweat was the national virtue.

When Jimmie arrived at the door, Newby himself looked up and could be seen to take fright and then cover it, pretending to have a piece of trash in his eye.

"Christ, what yer doing here?"

One of the sons stretched and yawned with fists extended;

76

then surveyed Jimmie without interest, and picked up a shovel.

"Yer know I haven' got anythink t' eat, boss. Yer know that."

"I can't go on f'wardin' yer supplies. The way yer working now."

"It isn't f'warding. I already earned everythink yer give me."

"Look, yer aren't working as good as yer did before them others came. Yer giving signs of giving up the job. Then I'll have all the expense and inconvenience of finding someone else."

"I already done nine hundred yards."

"Listen, Jimmie, don't come the bush-lawyer with me."

"I'm jest sayin'," Jimmie said, "I got a hungry wife and kid at home."

"She knows where she can come if she wants steady tucker. Miss Graf's made a generous offer."

"What offer?"

"Yer better ask Mrs Blacksmith."

"It ain't up to that bloody fat schoolteacher to make no offers."

The Newby boys stared narrowly at Jimmie and their father, defensive for the sake of their schoolmistress-lodger.

"Listen, yer black bastard!" Newby was saying. "Don't talk to me like that. I'll soon bloody . . ."

All at once, Jimmie had the rifle against Newby's stomach. Triumphant, Newby then seemed; as if *that* bullet were his ambition. The odds-on bet he had placed, in bedroom and kitchen conversation, with all the Newbys and the Friday wiseacres in Gilgandra, had come off in the end: Jimmie had shown his native malice.

Meanwhile, Jimmie cool-headedly chose not to shoot Newby. He took the muzzle away from Mr Newby's belly.

"That settles it, yer sodding darkie. Go home and straight t' bed. We'll talk about what's to be done t'morrow."

"Yair, we'll talk."

"One thing. You and yer bloody tribe are going t' pack up and git."

Secure about his wife and big-beamed daughters, he shut Jimmie and Tabidgi out.

Now Jimmie himself knew that Newby was not what he wanted. He was in a fever for some definite release. Killing Newby, however, was not it. When he put his rifle against Newby's gut, he knew that he wished to kill that honey-smooth Miss Graf. His desire for her blood, he understood, came as a climax to his earlier indecencies—relinquishing Harry Edwards to Senior Constable Farrell, for example. He wished to scare the schoolmistress apart with his authority, to hear her whimper.

In our world, the delusions that killers let into their blood-streams are the stuff of newsprint and videotape. A reader should be spared. Enough to say: Jimmie admitted to his body a drunken judgmental majesty, a sense that the sharp-edged stars impelled him. He felt large with a royal fever, with re-birth. He was in the lizard's gut once more.

There was little besotted about Tabidgi's sense of direction. He knew with a groan that they had turned for the main homestead once more.

"Yer not goin' back t' see the ole girl agin?" he complained.

"I got t' give them whites a scare."

"Christ Ormighty," the old man groaned. He laughed a little at all this commuting. He began to chant at random, for boredom and weariness.

> *Men vault rivers,*
> *Fear in their eyes.*
> *Women surrender.*
> *At dawn we are beyond your hill*
> *At midday we stalk you on tip-toe from a distance.*
> *At dusk we are at your throat,*
> *Closer than child to pap.*

This time the Newby woodheap got between them and the kitchen lights. A full-sized axe as well as a neater toma-hawk or block-buster were sunk into the wood. Jimmie propped his rifle there. An axe was more apt. He eased the cutting edges out of the hardwood block and told his uncle to hide the block-buster under his coat, and then sent him off to the door for one last, formal tempting of white contumacy.

78

"Chris' why?" Jackie asked but obeyed. There was so much he did not understand about the white world, and perhaps the reasons for carrying a concealed chopper under your coat while interviewing a farmer's wife were beyond his mental strength.

Out in the dark, Jimmie watched his uncle knock at the door and tell Mrs Newby that Mr Newby wanted them to be given flour.

"Did he give yer a note?" she asked.

"He was too busy, missus."

"D'yer expect me to go traipsing off to the old homestead to find out whether yer lying or not?"

"Tell him t' go away, Mum," the elder daughter called from indoors.

"Git yer rifle," the second one suggested.

There was a second's pause, then Mrs Newby turned from the door, perhaps to do as her daughter had urged. In the dark twenty yards out, lithe Jimmie thought explicitly how strange it was that she would never complete such a simple action, a robust woman with plenty of breath and deep red organs.

He thought so under cover of the axe, which was for him more than a mere cutting edge, was replete with command.

Out of the dark he ran yelping at her. Her hand was on the rifle and she was turning to shoot when the axe reached for her. It took her above the shoulder blade and mined the deep sinews there.

All the women in the kitchen commenced to scream, while Mrs Newby fell away from the axe. Jimmie vaulted her and waited on his light feet for Miss Graf to break from her warm corner by the hearth. Though one of the daughters ran towards her mother and perhaps the firearm, Jimmie Blacksmith did nothing to prevent her, and then chopped Miss Graf leisurely between hip and ribs.

As he struck and kept striking, Jimmie learned the ease of killing. People wrongly saw it as such extreme, terrifying work.

A second murderous theorem: the rate at which dignity could be severed. He had imagined Miss Graf playing somehow the cool moral arbiter to the end. To be raucous as a beast was more than he had hoped for from her.

Unreasonably, she rose to walk, below apprehending that he had knocked apart her rib cage and split her hams.

At the same time, he was aware of what Jackie was suffering, and what others were suffering from Jackie. Blood and screaming and starting eyes had stampeded the old man. Jackie would go on hacking at them out of terror. The horror Jimmie's first blow had made of Mrs Newby could only be fought with more and more blows.

One of the daughters too had become terrible, for by accidental mastery, Tabidgi had cut off her right hand.

The youngest son, eleven years old, came into the kitchen in a flannel nightgown. It occurred to Jimmie, drunk as he might be with insights, that Jackie Smolders would attack the child merely for horror of its eyes.

Jimmie yelled something preventive to his uncle, but Jackie was fighting demons and did some damage to the back of the boy's neck; who struggled for balance, hurdled his mother's body and sprinted out into the dark.

Within seconds, the yelling had strangely diminished to that of one of the daughters, who was sitting on her hips trying to rise. Behind her screams could be heard the sobbing of the child in its cot.

Jackie went on beating at the silent body of the other grown daughter, whose head lay half-scalped on her mother's lap. The juxtaposition looked like a mockery of a family-picnic photograph.

Mr Jimmie Blacksmith rolled on his feet and chopped off the back of the remaining Miss Newby's head. The axe was flecked with the strange grey mucus of the brain.

The sudden silence was enhanced rather than intruded on by the sobbing child, who sounded quotidian, likely to be taken by sleep at any moment.

Jimmie was frankly astounded at this instant absence of all enemy voices. How could he believe that Miss Graf's monumental concern over his marriage to Gilda had been removed from the earth?

Shivering Jackie Smolders had himself propped against the wall. Sweat shone in the grey stubble of his jaws. He had let his weapon drop amongst the slaughtered Newbys.

80

Though he felt buoyant enough, Jimmie Blacksmith knew that he had become an incurable. He knew in an instant that he must see into his acts the fervid illusions they were based on. He chose therefore to know and not go mad.

At the same time he must be able to see the four hewn women as culprits, and so the mere beginnings of an agenda of mayhem. Yet to see them fully and without doubt as the first necessary casualties of a war regally undertaken was itself a mad act of the mind.

Therefore he was to spend the rest of his life in tenuous elation and solid desolation between self-knowledge and delirium.

But at first the illusion, and the brain-heat from the killings, swallowed him whole, or nearly whole. He knew, without knowing he knew, how meanwhile to keep some cool true planet winking far out in his brain.

But the illusion must be tested against the fact of the women's bodies.

Somehow he was pleased to see that one of Mrs Newby's arms was moving, that the elder girl's face was composed and free of blood. Unfairly, she looked country-sweet, innocent of venom.

The younger lay on her side and like a person felled in midstride. Blood was splashed before and behind her, as if as a result of her own momentum.

Then Miss Graf. Her light-brown hair. The split bowl of her belly was in shadow.

The inspection took a little less than five seconds and was accomplished by small jolts of the head. He took Mrs Newby's rifle and roused Jackie to give it to him. But Jackie, already bedevilled, would not take it.

In the same corner as the rifle was a well-used hessian bag —possibly bedding for some household pet, deceased or wandered off. Jimmie shook it out and within half a minute or so had tipped into it some flour, beef, lard, bacon, bread, treacle, biscuit and rice—more or less Gilda's grocery list for the day. There was freedom for movement in that diagonal of the room. Most of the killing had been done in the opposite corner and against the front wall.

Ammunition for his and Mrs Newby's rifle was in the

81

dresser and he threw the cartridges in with the food bought that afternoon in the quiet town of Gilgandra.

From a roof hook hung a hand of Queensland bananas. He would march into Queensland, he promised himself. He might live in a cave and raise the boy to be a rebel.

Insanely he took a single banana into the hallway and found the bedroom where the child was weeping.

"Hungry," the small girl said. "I were hungry."

"There yer are, old girl," Jimmie said, in the almost Cockney accent of the aborigine speaking English. He gave her the fruit for comfort.

Somewhere in the dark her damaged brother reeled towards old Newby. But Jimmie was the master. In him the night was vested, and the gift of swift action. He decided he should enjoy it while it was there, this possession and being possessed.

9

THE BLACKSMITHS and Tabidgi and Peter fled east in the dark, over the open pastures of sheep farmers, important men, squatters. Like responsible travellers they closed the long, whining pasture gates behind them.

Tabidgi, cunning enough not to forget the port bottle, was yet incoherent, shrieking now and then in his derangement. "*Ghosts started by my hand,*" he would mumble,

> *Spirits fleeing back to their totem fathers,*
> *My barbs deep in their bodies,*
> *Come not near me.*
> *Here in the night I reign,*
> *Bullawi the great lizard,*
> *Whose scream shakes the hills apart.*

Mort and the girl had been told that there had been a battle and some of the Newbys hurt. They were promised more detail later, when they had built up a distance between Wallah and themselves.

What was she doing, the girl asked herself, fleeing by night with black men? Apart from being afraid of contradicting Jimmie in his battle flush, she was expiating for having borne the wrong child. And then there was fear of charity, Miss Graf's charity or the high, butterfly-collared, chaste-camisoled charity she had known as a child.

For Mort, there was duty towards wronged kin, Jimmie

Blacksmith, whose mood was valiant, the mood of a man grandly misused. Morton Blacksmith felt enlarged, escaping across a landscape barred by strangers' fences. To him, Tabidgi's yammering was nearly funny.

The girl wept a great deal, her arms ached, but the baby slept and murmured in its sleep. Mort laughed as Jackie continued to shriek his warning against spirits. The misery of Jackie Smolders' situation was that he had hacked and thwacked women dead because their screams had frightened him, but now he was frightened of silence. But Mort could not know this.

North of east, Jimmie knew, a knot of forested mountains travelled deep into the plains. Beyond their crest were places where he had been lusty and (he had once thought) clever. Queensland remained an abstract haven. There would be time to strike out for such a place.

In the meantime, he moved in a slumber of the limbs, a returning suspension of effort which he had lost through all his barter and contracting and which had come back to him now (he must pretend) as a reward for his work on the Newbys.

At miserable first light, seven hours after their march began, Jimmie Blacksmith let them rest. Gilda watched her husband and Mort conspiring, staring at old Jackie Smolders who was hugging a wet tree, retching, and falling at last into a coughing bundle. The frosted leaf-mould went black where his body rolled. It was a cold morning.

Are they planning to kill us? she wondered. Why should they? Why should they not? She could not move any more, and mentally bid Jimmie Blacksmith welcome to her life and even to the boy's.

The child, however, woke and called for the breast. She sat in a spiny embrasure of myrtle-tree roots and unbuttoned her breast, draping a blanket for modesty over her left arm. The vaporous cold grabbed at her nipple, but then the child found it and took nourishment.

"Little man," she said. "Poor little man. Yer should be much more black. Oh yairs yer should, yer villain, much more black."

So she fell asleep.

Jimmie gave Mort his knife and told him to go down and kill some farmer's sheep. It was safer, more sensible, to take fresh meat now, while they travelled in advance of the news of what had been done at Newby's.

Mort slung the sheep-skin over a fence, happy in service of his brother.

"Old Newby and his sons said we could starve," Jimmie had confided to Mort. "So we took to 'em with axes."

Which accounted for the clotted state of Tabidgi's trouser ankles. Old Tabidgi could be expected to stumble about at the honest business of killing those who denied due food.

Laughing benevolently, Mort woke Gilda from a two-hour sleep, and held tea close to her dazed face.

"Yer better tuck up, missus," he told her. "Too bloody cold."

The frost was still on the ground, and the first day of Jimmie Blacksmith's new era sat greyly beneath the trees, and Jackie Smolders repented in crazy monotones in the place where he had fallen.

But, above his simous nose broken in play, Peter's wide-awake eyes seemed to be expecting damage. Gilda did not care to look at him for long.

When Jimmie strode up to her, rifle slung over his elbow, an ungovernable flush of brood heroism caused her to cover the child with her body.

"D'yer think I'd do anythink like that?" he asked.

"I dunno, Jimmie."

"Listen, we got t' keep on now. Let yer go soon. You and the littl'un. How's he?"

"He's feedin' well. Real well. And he slep' well."

"Righto."

"Jimmie?"

"Yair?"

"I don' care if yer shoot me fer sayin' it." But she had to take this, one of the rare times since the birth that Jimmie had spoken to her directly, not obliquely, by way of the child or of a piece of furniture. "I really thought the baby was yores. I really thought. I should've thought it might of been that other feller's. But I really truly thought it was yores."

Jimmie Blacksmith looked at the pale jaws and the mouth that tended to hang open; at the bun she had made of her variably grey-brown hair; at her damp straw hat and charity-case top-coat of navy serge slung like a tent over the childishness of her body.

It frightened him that he wanted to forgive her and talk of the slaveries they each had suffered. It might happen to be one of the strict rules of self-balance that if he saw Gilda Howie as victim today he might see Miss Graf in the same light tomorrow. She should, by the rules, be a kind of enemy but her paltry face and sharp shoulders were inadequate to the role. Perhaps she was her own special case and quite safe to pity. He didn't know and didn't feel like taking risks.

"If yer think anyone cheated me, yer kin tell the p'lice. They'll ask yer a lot about me and yer kin tell 'em."

They marched for another hour.

Jackie Smolders, Mungindi elder and cherisher of enchanted teeth, had given up. He had seen four women's blood, when the sighted blood of one was sufficient to bring on catastrophe. He had laboured in the potent blood of women's throats and hacked-out wombs. He closed his eyes and blood slanted in torrents across the darkness behind his lids.

"Jimmie," the white girl, heels blistered, called aloud to her husband. "Jimmie, for pity's sake!"

Until the sun was high in the north, he ignored her. Then he told them all to rest and began himself to cook a forequarter of the carcass Mort had butchered, quickly bled and cheerfully carried all morning.

Tabidgi was in the mood for dying, but innocent enough to believe it could be induced in the old way, by acceptance of omens.

Jimmie came down to Gilda and the baby. He had dropped everything, his load of food, his rifle.

"I goin' t' take yer t' the Dubbo road. Yer'll git rescued by a farmer or somethink. Tell the p'lice I said I declared war. Tell 'em about how bloody measly Newby was. Tell 'em all the damage done at Newby's I did, not Tabidgi. And I declared war. Orright?"

"Yairs, Jimmie." In the joy of escaping him she could pity him and even put out a hand, as if to pat his face. But his eyes blinked, warning her off tenderness.

"I'll carry the little'un for yer."

"No, it's orright."

"Christ, he was almost mine. Let me bloody carry him."

It was as well, for most of the mile-and-a-half they walked was uphill, sown with boulders; then down through a wooded defile to the Dubbo road, as Jimmie had promised.

"Make his bloody father give him a help in life," he advised Gilda and gave the child back to her.

Jimmie looked back on her from the top of the defile. She had seated herself cross-leggedly, with care, on the grass verge. She looked pitiably open for all the fresh miseries that would roll in on her with the creak of a farmer's dray.

In late afternoon they had to leave mumbling Jackie Smolders and the boy Peter on a tributary road with meat and tea to last them the day. The boy was schooled to announce Jackie Smolders' innocence to all comers. Contrite, tender, guilty—all these Jimmie could have felt for Jackie Smolders, who had come to him for honest reasons of kin and tribal sorcery and cash for liquor. But he could sense how unprofitable they would be. It was, in any case, impossible to talk to the old man.

Jimmie was delighted to be finished with all but his gay, misinformed, fast, muscular brother. Now fast, craftsman-like tracks could be made. They dragged boughs behind them. High up in the Divide they came to someone's unprofitable boundary fence, post-and-rail. Gripping the shaggy-grained upper rail with one hand, they walked crabwise along it for close on a mile. The exercise became painful. The rifles slung from their necks hunched them further into a posture of discomfort. But Mort enjoyed it all, the times this or that item threatened to fall.

Further up still, beyond anyone's thirst for property, they made a fire and rolled themselves in their blankets.

At midnight cold and hunger woke them. Before dawn they crossed the central spur of the Divide and when the sun began to give warmth, wrapped themselves in their blankets and slept till the early afternoon of Sunday.

Already Jimmie found it hard to believe in the slaughter of the Newbys. It had become remote, like an alien truth, like the story of how the Red Sea was crossed.

Pursuit too was hard enough to believe in in the still, high forest.

Forty-five miles to the south-west, preachers were reading

their various Sunday prefigurements into what had been done at the Newby homestead.

Jimmie loved living cleanly with his brother in the forest, feared losing Mort; yet understood that he might corrupt the boy by not confessing to the murder of women, by not sending him away. For there was no question that the blood of women overrode all kinship loyalty, and yet that he himself must keep to a reprisal list if his soul were not to freeze about the cold fact of the Newby killings.

Mort must either be incriminated for fear of losing him or lost for fear of incriminating him. While Jimmie could not have said it in such abominably neat terms, he could feel the actual prongs of the question turning in his flesh.

Shattered Mrs Newby lived for three days and said that it was the old one who had done her most damage.

Attending doctors were awed by the magnificence of her will towards life. The police paid sombre compliments to the explicit quality of her evidence. Women wept at her clear-headed mourning of her daughters and the esteemed Miss Graf.

Her dying was grand; it was royal and saintly, outscaling her weekly cheese-paring in Gilgandra, her bullying of Gilda, to an extent that Jimmie Blacksmith would have considered unjust.

Mr Newby was tranced. Farmers who had come to offer services to the police kept drugging him from flasks of rum and whisky.

Through the fug of sympathetic liquors, he remembered and wondered how he had ever forgotten that when he had first come to the west as an eighteen-year-old from Dorset he had seen and been numbed by its air of withdrawal, as if it had vast dispassionate and random devilries beneath its crust. Yet it had become his home, nearer to him than his heart's blood. He did not know how he had ever settled to it. He knew he would sell up now and perhaps go into business in Sydney. To his mind, the earth and Jimmie Blacksmith had become suddenly allied.

The elder of the two grown sons had been the first to go into the kitchen. He rode off to Gilgandra where there were three doctors. What he needed were people to say yes, they are horrifically dead; and country policemen to tell him yes, this is the worst outrage.

All day Saturday and Sunday women—the women whose men brought flasks—brought cakes, made continual tea for policemen, doctors, mourners, condolers, and served it in Mrs Newby's china.

The Newby boys were still talkative. Still they wanted to speak of what it had been like before blankets and scouring brushes had been brought into play. They were insatiable for words like *monstrous, unspeakable, black butchers.*

"After all Dad did for them bastards," the younger son said, and the sentiment was passed from mourner to mourner.

At mid-afternoon on Saturday, the first party of police and volunteers rode out of the homestead yard. Men raised their hats and wished them well as they rode towards the Blacksmith encampment to pick up a track. The clever full-blood who was the Gilgandra tracker circled the site once and could then point out the traces made in flight. These pointed east.

"His people live over that way," the policeman told the volunteers.

All felt that an arrest was close.

Early on Monday morning, Dowie Stead, lately Miss Graf's fiancé, informed of the sad demise by telegraph, rode up to the Newby homestead leading five friends, young farmers from Gulargambone.

The friends varied, for Dowie was secretly romantic and practically tough. So he had both an orotund Irish-Australian called Toban and the impermeable good sense of a squatter-bachelor of thirty-five whose name was Dud Edmonds.

They had all drunk rum with their breakfast: it aided their air of concerted outrage.

As young Mr Dowie Stead, alone of the six, dismounted, a farmer's wife was cooking breakfast for the Newby men.

Another fed the four-year-old in the corner, making weaving gestures with the spoon to amuse the child, whose laughter ran thinly in the great kitchen.

Dowie Stead looked like a national product, a tall boy with brown hair and narrow blue eyes; a face full of rather passive good intentions with a sort of Nordic coldness to it; features a little small for such a big frame yet likely to be more poetic or downright pretty if the proportion had been better arranged.

There was a functionality about his body; and people knew, having beaten drought and fluke, grasshoppers and banks to own what they owned, that functionality mattered.

It comforted them to see him.

Mr Newby, drinking whisky neat with his tea, was pleased to see him, and, with a tenderness Dowie found awesome, poured one for him. Mr Newby clearly presumed Dowie was half as shattered as himself. The young squatter felt some embarrassment that he was not. He drank quickly, since that might convince the Newbys how much he needed soothing and might also help him work up some sentimentality for the girl's memory.

"Your intended was a beautiful girl," said Mr Newby, and gave a strange little giggle of sobs.

One of the Newby boys said, "After all Dad done for them."

"The little girl's orright?"

"Yair. She was asleep in her cot. She had a banana skin with her. One of the girls . . . or Mrs Newby . . . must've given it to her not long before . . ."

Mr Newby took a steadying handful of the table and snorted up his grief.

"Her face wasn't hurt at all, your intended's," the elder Newby boy told Dowie.

"How's Mrs Newby?"

"The doctor says she'll pass away today."

"It'll be a mercy."

"The youngest boy's orright. Except he seen it all happen. He heard the bastards calling to each other while they . . ."

Dowie Stead should have felt vastly angered. Instead he felt elected to give chase. This sense of election outweighed his guilt at feeling no grief of his own; which lack of response —he believed—was a judgment on him for rolling lubras in Gulargambone.

It did not fully occur to him yet that he might not have loved Miss Graf, for everybody said she was good and wise and handsome. Like Gilda, Dowie had always been awed by her. It worried him that he was lightened every time he remembered that now he did not have to marry her.

In fact, he looked forward to travelling with friends, harbouring a simple ambition, eating and sleeping in the open. Miss Graf's tortuous standards of refinement had been swept away—or rather, hacked apart—and now he was with men, their direct, brusque warmth, all aimed at repaying someone for her outlandish agonies.

In Gulargambone he had cashed a cheque for sixty pounds at the Squatters' Club. Today he wondered whether he should not take out a new, blue-hatched five-pound note and say that he would not cease the hunt until he had rinsed it in Jimmie Blacksmith's blood. It was a little wild and imaginative, and Dowie was not at all sure that it should be done. But it might soothe the Newbys, who were bona fide mourners.

Mrs Newby, however, died during the inquest, making the gesture inappropriate.

Towards the end of the sitting a post office clerk arrived from Dubbo with a telegraph message that Jackie Smolders had been found and taken to Dubbo. The news threw the inquiry out of stride. One of the monsters had been taken inadvertently, behind their backs. Farmers gurgled approval but were a little deflated.

But the coroner himself, stressing that he made the point in an unofficial way, said the genuine devil was Jimmie Blacksmith, who, by report, considered himself at war and who could only be found by dedicated means.

Twenty more men offered themselves for a week as mounted auxiliaries to the police.

That very Monday Dowie Stead's party rode off independently, though in the established easterly direction.

Dowie was not at peace with himself. Ridiculously he had a hunger for a thin, consumptive black girl called Tessie. For him, Tessie was a passion. Desire always came to him in her form—a lazy, gristly dying girl who yet had a sumptuous impact.

But the obsession with Tessie had more to it than lust; Dowie could not cease to worry at her image.

Because, reeling from the Squatters' Club to his horse one Saturday night and so to the blacks' camp, he had brought Tessie moon-eyed to the door of her humpy, barring entry. He forced past her. On her mattress sat his father in shirt-tails.

If now there was anything he wanted to pay off the black race for, it was not killing Miss Graf, canonized already by the people of Wallah and rendered remote in the process. It was for bringing his father and himself, both unbuttoned and grotesquely ready for the same black arse, face to face.

In Balmain, a riverside suburb of the city of Sydney, the public hangman for the State of New South Wales kept a scrupulous butchery. There were clean sawdust on the floor each day, a capacious coolroom and two polite sons. He himself was an exemplary man, full of placid love. Three mornings a week he or one of his sons bought carcasses at the Homebush slaughteryards. He was at his most talkative on meat: he would pick up lumps of sirloin and praise their texture before housewives.

His name was Wallace Hyberry. He lacked intimate friends so that he was never called anything more colloquial than Wallace—he remained Wallace, in fact, amongst a race of Wallys. The ladies of Balmain thought he was refined, almost like some of the foreign gentlemen in the hair shops in town.

They all knew he was the public hangman and said they couldn't imagine him hanging a soul.

Though he was called the "public" hangman, hangings had not been public in that State since a day sixty years before when a convicted outlaw urged the onlookers to turn on every bloody tyrant in the budding Britannic colony.

So necrophiles like Ted Knoller, a customer Mr Hyberry could have lost without regret, had to be content with newspaper reports and with buying their meat from the hangman himself.

Late on the Monday, the day news of the Newby shambles appeared in the press, Knoller came to the butchery. He always carried a note listing the meat needs of the Knoller house, and would stand at the back of the shop against the tiles, making patterns in the sawdust with his boots and motioning women to give Mr Hyberry their order before he should.

Mr Hyberry would work tight-lipped on the meat while Knoller was there. Tidy, efficient, with a sense of social duty, he did not think it fair to have his highest contribution to society, the painless-as-possible extinction of murderers, slavered over by a cracked navvy, relished like an obscenity.

At last there was only a sixty-year-old deaf lady buying cat-meat, and Knoller began on the atrocity of the Friday night before, reading details aloud from the *Morning Herald*.

"I know that area well," he said. "I'm a Gilgandra boy meself. I might know these Newby people. Though I can't exactly remember . . . Anyhow, the *Mail*'ll have all the photographs."

Mr Hyberry cut fillets with his fine-honed knife. "Surely not *all*, Mr Knoller. There are some things the public ought to be spared."

"How d'yer mean?"

"Murder isn't just a matter of being made to lie down on the floor. Even virgins and wives can die in ways that make the toughest policeman sick. There would have been photographs taken far too terrible for anyone other than doctors and senior policemen to look at."

Ted Knoller frowned to imply he hoped he would never be forced to see anything that was not decent.

"I wouldn't want t' see nothink like that. What I mean was I might reckernize the farm or some of the people "

"Oh yes."

It was a pleasure to see Mr Hyberry at work on sirloin. Half a dozen slittings with the knife, then thump, thump, thump with the cleaver down the lines of cleavage. Behold, seven portions of meat fell from his scrubbed hand onto the marble of the scale.

"What strikes me," Knoller pursued him, "is this. This morning there's news of a really bad murder. Yer just in the same position I am. Yer don't know the killers, and yer don't know those poor women who got killed. Jimmie Blacksmith's a name yer never heard of. But now yer know yer going t' meet him on the gallows. For the final act in a killing that'll always be remembered. Yer got a ringside seat to history! . . . I mean, it must be an interesting thing t' know that all the famous murderers, when they get caught, have got t' face you in the end."

"I don't face them. I don't say a word to them. I'm just part of the . . . apparatus."

A bad silence began. Hyberry's industrious sons kept working. Knoller could not stop sneering, hinting that there was surely a morbidity in the hangman to keep his own company. Hyberry was a prude. If he himself had been hangman he would have been happy to pass on little intuitions and professional yarns. It must all have its humorous side.

Mr Knoller, living in terror of death, was very interested in its humorous side. He began to niggle the butcher, from a new direction.

"Anyhow, these Blacksmiths are aborigines. I believe blacks present problems."

"How do you mean?"

"I mean ordinary problems. *Scientific* problems, yer might say. Problems with hanging, yer know."

"I didn't know. I'd better leave such questions to you, Mr Knoller, since you are the expert."

"Well, that last black yer hanged. In Bathurst. I don't like to say it, but the newspapers did."

"They said what?"

"That he nearly got his head pulled off."

Mr Hyberry shuddered but showed no fear. Hanging was a trade for which there could be no apprenticeship. One only got one's craft bit by bit and in the practice itself.

So that when you hanged a thin aboriginal man, an old man almost, and the rope savaged and part-severed the thin neck at the end of the fall, then you learned more about weight, age, momentum.

But he had a furious contempt for people who passed on such stories.

"What newspapers said that?"

"*Truth* and the *Sporting Chronicle*."

"What's a sporting paper doing, printing that sort of stuff?"

Mr Knoller shrugged. "Have yer got any decent blade steak?" he wanted to know, as if it was Hyberry who had been delaying *him* with abominations.

10

B Y NOW the Blacksmith brothers had crossed to the rainy side of the mountains. Dying trees wore long mosses, the tree ferns were tall, and underfoot was deep lush mould full of prosperous insects. All of the Monday and Tuesday a small belt of thunderheads moved with them, continually soaking.

They had powers of instinct not only to resist but to ignore this. But Jimmie Blacksmith's mind itched with the quandary: whether to inform and free Mort or to corrupt and possess him. There was no hurry, he told himself, but knew that was not the truth. He had his list of enemies, and must move towards them in order. Otherwise, he fully understood, he might as well sit down and be contrite for the Newbys and Miss Graf.

Meanwhile, if Mort asked, he was favoured with lying details of the fight with the Newby men, which became more and more an exercise of honour, the sort of thing old war chants spoke of.

The wet blanket on Jimmie Blacksmith's shoulders itched as he lied and lied.

They found out they were carrying too much food. Having foraged for five people they were suddenly a sleek, a swift two. Now they dropped pounds of that Newby beef, snatched by Jimmie on the Friday night, into a steep gorge.

It was salutary to slough it off; they grinned a little at each other and felt well together. If events could only take Mort by the scruff of the neck and commit him to bloodiness but leave him sensible and full of good heart.

Jimmie himself still waited for the slump of spirits which could be expected after merciless Friday night. It failed to come. He was still in a viable balance between belief and non-belief in the dismembering he had done. At the same time, the thorough nature of the punishment he had dealt out continued to soothe and flatter him. Because he had been effective. He had actually manufactured death and howling dark for people who had such pretensions of permanence. He had cut down obelisks to white virtue. So, with his brain heaving in contrary directions, he was still largely light-hearted, and moved quickly in the irksome wet forest. He knew that he was on the same side of the mountains as some of his most cherished enemies.

Mrs Healy was worth remembering too, with something like a lover's remembrance. If *that* were a form of madness, then he welcomed it.

Meanwhile, what should be done with grinning Mort? Mort had suggestions of his own. It was Wednesday. A wind had come in from the north-east and turned the rain to squalls. Jimmie felt fevered: the bedding was very wet. All at once, Mort spoke of a timber-getter he had once worked with, a low Irishman called Mullett, a feller of cedar over in the direction of the Barrington Tops. Mullett lived well, being a single man, who could usually find some genial female relic to live there with him up in the lush forests fifteen miles or so from where they stood, splashed and gusted.

The timberman could also be trusted to have warming spirits in the house and would not have heard of the Wallah murders; not that he could be relied on to care if he had.

Late on an afternoon of blinding headwinds, they crossed the railway two miles east of the Merriwa terminus and, in case their tracks be found, walked four or five furlongs westward on the rails before turning north for Mullett's place. Where the sleepers stood up well from the rail-bed they hopped from one to the other but for at least a few hundred yards, where the track had sunk a little into its matrix soil, walked the one wet blue rail, arms out, rifle in the left hand balancing gunny-sack in the right. By these means, even a good tracker, and all those who waited for his reading of the signs, could be held up for hours.

Head-on into the gale, the Blacksmith boys walked more than twenty-five miles in hope of Mullett's hospitality. They scarcely spoke. Morton Blacksmith did not laugh now when anything was dropped, but navigated truly through the solid drench.

Near dusk they saw the lights and heard the groan of a sawmill on their right. Then the oozing dark came down. They must steal a hurricane lamp, thought Jimmie. The wet brush spanked their thighs. They must steal oilskins.

Two hours later, Mort pointed to Mullett's light. The approach was up an avenue long ago cleared by drag-log, partly overgrown now with young trees. Thirty yards from the front door stood a stupendous cedar trunk. Its chopping platform remained, to give it the look of a memorial.

Mort fell against the door and beat at it. At last it was opened by someone out of sight, probably Mullett's woman. Small, wild-eyed, with ponderous moustaches, the lumber-man himself stood framed, holding a very old musket by its long barrel.

"Mullett, yer mad bastard. It's Mort Blacksmith! And me brother, Jimmie."

Mullett blinked. "I haven' got much food in, yer know."

The brothers felt deprived of the gushing Irish welcome Mort had promised. To Jimmie, even the way the man spoke his Irish was like Healy's, with a narrow thrifty sound to it.

"We brung all our food," Mort sang. "We jest want t' sleep in front of yer fire. We bin goin' all day. Blankets've got all wet."

"Yair. Well, welcome to yer. Come on in out of the wet."

It was warm in Mullett's hut. With a high opinion of his own slyness the host brought from a hiding place a stone jar of overproof rum. But Jimmie Blacksmith did not respond to it; he was bent on storing away the benefits of warmth, light, shelter.

On the other hand, Mort drank a lot, as did Mullett and the girl. Within an hour Mort and the young lady were jigging while Mullett played a mouth organ. In this area he was highly accomplished and his eyes gleamed at the end of tunes, when he knocked the instrument into his cupped hand to beat the spittle from it. Mort sang over and over again a song called "My Black-eyed Kittie".

"Where yer both off to?"

"We in trouble with the p'lice."

"Yer don't tell me."

"Yair. We goin' t' go to Queensland."

"Bloody Queensland? What'd yer do?"

"Killed couple'r ewes."

"Yer don't tell me? What p'lice is after yer?"

"Gilgandra p'lice."

"God, but yer put some daylight between them and yer-selves!"

By then, the spit had been knocked out of Mullett's harmonica. The big sweating girl was ready again to jig.

Jimmie Blacksmith wondered if Mullett and Mort might not come to conflict over the bumpkin girl, little as she was worth it. But he was wisely asleep before the question came to trial.

He was tempted to stay another night under Mullett's shelter. But people who did not know this morning of the killings might by evening. News of the murder of women would travel days faster, counties ahead of the newspapers. So they must leave and get used to being at war with the entire human landscape.

And he had easterly enemies to strike, and the puzzlement over Mort to resolve, not to be considered in Mullett's rowdy hovel.

In new sunlight they marched slantwise down the valley. The nearer they came to Healy's, the easier the profile of the country they crossed. They moved, mainly under cover, on the northern rim of the dairy and orchard country. When they got to Healy's, Mort had been told, Jimmie would demand just compensation.

About midday they saw a man driving a horse-drawn harrow. His back was to them and his knobbly, veined, industrious elbows. For a second Jimmie Blacksmith considered shooting him, bringing to an end an individual history of white thrift and penny-wisdom and mistrust. But *that* was too fanciful a gesture.

Having fenced it himself, he knew Healy's boundary. In fields which had been fallow when Jimmie had last been there, tall corn crops masked their approach to the homestead. They came diagonally across a cornfield, Mort in his bare feet. They could hear the panic of wintering snakes, and grain rats slithering off through the tall stooks.

Jimmie had known that if he delayed speaking straight to Mort, responsibility would shift. Mort would catch the passion or see that anyone who has loaded weapons is only a hair away from savagery; and that therefore he is still human, and in need of kin, if the hair snaps.

It was at the second when, parting the grain, they saw Healy's sleek home, pastures and fat grazing cows that Jimmie Blacksmith knew that he had not come so much to repay Healy, unless Healy happened to be at home. It was the spacious wife he had travelled for. He could, in fact, sense her at the glowing heart of the house.

God help Mort and him. He was mad. He had become a woman-killer, given over to the bad prefiguration of women's blood. Lush Mrs Healy was waiting to be split apart, as Petra Graf had waited.

"Run away, Mort," he suddenly said. "Run right away, for sweet Jesus' sake."

"Yer only come here t' git justice."

"No, run away. I don't want yer help. Bugger off. Please."

Mort laughed, more like the old Mort than at any time in the last week. He was beseeched to flee at the risky top of Jimmie's voice but went on chucklng in the old Mort way.

Jimmie resorted to Mungindi for greater force.

"There is a woman here, fat as a grub. She is a devil woman and put magic on your kinsman so that he writhed and shivered to the edge of death. She has bewitched her husband. She is the fang of the coiled adder."

"Yair?" Mort smirked, not understanding. "There ain't no cure fer that sort of bitch."

Jimmie gave up and broke from Healy's crops, across a fence, and sprinted for the farmhouse door. He could not, however, outdistance Mort's terrible loyalty.

So that Mort was, in fact, closer to the doorway when a gaunt, confused lady of about forty years appeared there with a level rifle. The rattle of Mort's foot on the veranda boards caused Mrs Healy to utter a full creamy yelp inside the house. Hearing it, Jimmie stopped and shivered with his peculiar lunacy. The gaunt lady fired and the bullet, he later decided, must have passed between the hang of his left arm and his side.

Instantly Mort shot the woman high upon the right of her chest. The impact sat her suddenly flat on the boards.

How distressed Mort was! He knelt by the woman, unable to believe in the rough bloody damage he had done her. He had not learned that a person catches deadliness as a disease is caught.

There was no time to console Mort with the awful dicta of atrocity. Mr Jimmie Blacksmith stepped over the threshold.

Mrs Healy stood up, grunting terror through her full lips. She had a baby in her arms, in a long, trailing shawl. An inheritor for Healy. Healy chose to have an inheritor, the cook not to. Choice was too bloody easy for them.

It was like the positioning of stars: the baby seemed to swing into a phase where it was germane to his lust for Mrs Healy's lightly creased, tall, shrieking throat.

Jimmie raised his rifle and sighted it beneath her full-contoured jaw.

"Yer fuckin' husband wouldn' even give me a ride into Merriwa," Jimmie reminisced.

Outside, Mort was comforting the felled mother's-aide. "It's jest twenty-two gauge," he consoled her. She stared ahead of her with a look of mild bemusement on her face. Her hands were beginning to turn blue.

Mrs Healy ran to the dresser corner, where she did not fit neatly because of her hips. As she turned, Jimmie shot her in the throat. There was one terrible flush of blood across the floor, then she sank and died in the corner.

Everything was compulsion now. He was standing above the baby who had remained enshawled on Mrs Healy's lap.

"Father's little joy!" he reproached it, weeping loudly.

Mort called to him from the door, but he was already reloaded and fired at the child's head, keeping his eyes shut tight.

When Jimmie Blacksmith opened his eyes, Mort was kneeling beside the ruins of Mrs Healy and her child. Mort's face was as thick-featured and swollen as if he had wept for hours.

Jimmie Blacksmith returned to his practical, functioning body.

"Don't say I didn' tell yer to bugger off. I told yer and yer laughed."

"Healy deserve all this?" Mort asked thickly. There was no irony in him. He was silly with shock. He hoped that Jimmy would itemize Healy's guilt, to make it commensurate with the mess in the kitchen corner.

"He starved me and he told me bloody lies."

"But it's woman-blood." Mort screamed. "And it's child-blood."

"Don't yer worry yerself about that blood bullshit," said Jimmie as if Mort was distressed only on magical grounds. "Anyhow, she saw me walk all the way t' Merriwa and passed me by, sitting up in the dray."

"Jesus Christ, will yer look what yer done?"

"I know what I done." He slipped into Mungindi. "She tried to take my soul away from me. She had me bewitched and she'd do it again, I know she'd do it again. . . ." But he gave up and saw through the vacuum of the bereaved kitchen that the lady-companion was crawling on hands and knees, studiously, trying not to let her knees catch the fall of her dress short, for then the cloth might tug at her wound.

"Healy deserves to see his kid. And so does Gilda and . . . and all the friggin' others. Anyhow, the old girl's left yer a decent rifle."

He pointed out the weapon, abandoned on the veranda boards.

Improbably the woman continued, past the woodheap, bleeding onto the grass and blurring the patterns of her blood with the passage of her knees.

"Yer got a dinkum rifle now," he told Mort. Mort's eyes widened. They could not apprehend this woman- and child-killer, or how he had sprung up in the familiar features of his half-brother.

To the right of the homestead gate fine heifers were beginning to mill for milking. They ignored the arduously creeping lady-companion.

Meanwhile, Jimmie busied about looking for food and cartridges, while Mort sat weeping.

"Let's git away, Jimmie. Let's git away t' Queensland."

"Healy's got t' see this. This is all for Healy."

"I fort it was b'cause she wouldn't give yer a ride in a fuckin' dray," roared Mort.

"Jest sit there, Mort, and git it out of yer system. Yer weren't here in the first place. Yer don't know jest what these people did t' me."

All Mort did was lay his head down sideways on the kitchen table, his spatulate nose seeming further widened from his new acquaintance with horror. Half a dozen loud creaking sobs came out of him and moisture from his mouth ran onto Mrs Healy's sandsoaped country table.

When Jimmie paused in his busy ransacking it was to wonder if he should put a bullet into the doggedness of the lady-companion. It had brought her very close to the homestead gate.

But before she had got that far, Healy came riding up on a tall black horse with white facing. He was fully visible through the open kitchen door. In his hand was the second household rifle.

Jimmie backed to a front corner of the kitchen. "Jest let him have a good look at what he bloody caused."

Already Healy was out of the saddle and consulting the lady-companion. He laid her back to rest and came on with his rifle high, the butt at his right armpit.

Without warning Mort left the kitchen door, staggering comically, as if it were the old gay Mort miming, perhaps, drunken Jackie Smolders.

Even Healy was amazed, thinking either that Mort was wounded or mocking him or attracting his aim. At last the farmer fired, but at the very second Mort went into one of his arbitrary sidewise totters.

Healy's right hand was now in his pockets scrabbling for cartridges. Mr Jimmie Blacksmith stepped out into daylight and shot him through the heart.

Healy cheated once more. The big harsh man died touchingly as a saint. He dropped his rifle to one side, like a tool relinquished deliberately and with common sense. In the same second he knelt and made a deep salaam until his forehead touched the earth. Three seconds later he tipped sideways in this same posture, in which he had ridden in his mother's womb in 1854 in Sligo.

"Yer stupid bastard," Jimmie told his limp half-brother. "I wanted him to see what he bloody caused."

Mort it was, though, who was practical enough to go out across the moist black soil and proliferating grass to see if Healy was really gone. There was no doubt. He went on to the thin bitter lady he had shot and lifted her in his arms.

"Put me down," she said, "yer black devil."

Mort was too distressed to plead his goodwill.

"Yer'll hang for this, yer know. When they hang yer, remember how I predicted it."

Mort sobbed confirmatory sobs. The woman babbled away, short of breath but at length.

"And then yer'll go to deepest hell. Mr Healy went to Communion last Sunday and has been working long days ever since. He'll go to heaven and yer'll go to deepest hell."

"D'yer want a drink of water?" Mort pleaded. "And I'll wrap blankets round yer. It's only twenty-two gauge."

"Mr Healy knew yer were coming. But he didn't for a second b'lieve yer'd turn on her. On him, yairs. But on *her*!"

Indoors, Jimmie seemed scarcely uneasy after all his luxurious homicide and wanted something savoury. He had found a ginger-cake and come out, bulge-mouthed, waving wedges at his brother. He could easily have felt hollowness and boredom but still knew they were the luxuries of the repenter and the madman.

Somehow now, he must prop up Mort until Mort was reconciled enough to prop himself.

Meanwhile, as Mort ran about getting blankets and water for Mrs Healy's friend, Jimmie put on a harsh front. "Why don't yer run and fetch the p'lice as well?"

Jimmie promised. No more women, no more women. He felt secretly lightened in that no other woman on earth suggested herself as victim—not, anyhow, in the compelling manner of Mrs Healy and Miss Petra Graf. Not Mrs Hayes, certainly not Mrs Treloar.

At dusk, both brothers felt strangely exposed, as if the act of mayhem at Healy's had conveyed their names instantly to all the people of the area.

Lewis would be forewarned now, and Farrell too; Jimmie eagerly debated strategy with Mort. It's a war, he told Mort; if he, Jimmie Blacksmith, went to those who had wronged him and asked them like a gentleman to give his due to him, they'd laugh. And then he tried to convey to Mort how all they wanted from a black was foreseeable failure.

But no more women, Jimmie promised. No more women. Trying to restore Mort, he secretly let his mind run in splendid patterns, patterns close to dementia, patterns to besot yourself with. In the heart of house-proud Merriwa he would shoot down Farrell. All the women of the countryside would be in terror of his name; they would sweat palpable fear. He was a walking rape of womens' souls.

Yet he went on soberly swearing: no more women, Mort.

He let Mort have a little of the brandy he had taken from Healy's place, but not too much. For in the morning they must double back north-west and confuse their tracks.

Even after a warm portion of liquor, Mort painted his face with white clay before sleeping. So that spirits, especially those freshly started, suddenly unloosed, uncertain of night's profile, could not identify and latch on him.

In the morning it was Jimmie who woke heartsick. But his primal talent of navigation and speed over the ground, the numb, easy talents of the senses in contact with terrain, these restored him.

The journeying life, each camp no true point of arrival, braced him now that he had resigned from the white cycle, in which the ground is broken, the pod laid down and the seed puts out its roots.

They came close to Verona the next night and saw that mounted police had encamped there, at least fifteen. A black-tracker watered the horses from the camp tank, out of square, tea-tin buckets. His luck!

All the police could do, in the face of Jimmie's manifesto

of blood, was mill at places he had once been. The brothers sensed this, were heartened by it.

Again, that night, though they were miles on into the hills, they could not have a fire. Mort, however, was permitted the rest of the brandy. *"Here are we, Tullam men,"* Mort sang gently,

> *Dressed in the night,*
> *Dressed the grey hue of sleeping plants.*
> *Our shoulders press the wind towards newer moans,*
> *We are in its change of voice.*
> *Be careful and do not sleep,*
> *For nothing more terrible than Tullam man*
> *Will ever break the sleep of living man.*
> *Be careful,*
> *When the moon turns pale,*
> *It is for Tullam man.*
> *When stars run for the cover of thunderheads,*
> *It is for Tullam man. . . .*

Jimmie welcomed the song. It didn't sound like self-mockery. Perhaps it meant that Mort was trying to fit their movements into a tribal pattern.

For they saw salutary things that week, things to knit them closer. At the timber village of Borambil, high in the Divide, an armed picquet! Many families seemed to have moved into the school residence and post office, and children, even those too young for school, played in the schoolteacher's garden.

They were shot at while flanking in upon a scarcely habitable shanty in a clearing.

It was as if their story had turned a corner—first Jimmie's spree, then encouragement towards zeal for survival.

West again over the Divide, they found an empty house to steal from. Was it a Friday or perhaps a funeral? Though he might be a man who had killed women, Jimmie secretly fretted that it might be a funeral. It was not a rich man's hut, not the hut of an established man, but commodities were exactly laid out in it, all in order, the cups in the dresser, the wood in its box, the wick in the hurricane lamp white and precisely trimmed. A battler's house, not the house of the sort of man they had made war with. Jimmie didn't wish on its owner a funeral and a looting in the one day.

There were no newspapers for Jimmie to read what a plague he was.

As for Mort, he was restored and given new vigor by touching household things, tea canisters, sugar scoops, jam tins; even if it was only with the relative innocence of a thief that he touched them. He left the place tidy, at least, and there was no blood on the walls.

Dowie Stead thought of his comrades as a fast striking force, like the new striking forces that were being formed in South Africa to hunt the slithery Boer. By arriving at Healy's only the day after the Blacksmiths had been there they had proved their quality and had their sense of being the vengeance strengthened. Not that they were presented with the direct evidence of Jimmie Blacksmith's work. The coroner, wise enough to know that babies are powerful stimulants one way or another, and that this one would merely stimulate hysteria, sent a telegram that only first-degree relatives were to see the remains. So Dowie Stead had learned nothing at Healy's, nor from his conference with the lady-companion.

But while squadrons of Mounted Rifles, sent to Dubbo instead of Cape Town, encumbered the west, and parties of volunteers solemnly followed the Blacksmiths' cold spoor, *they* had been only a day behind the devil himself. That proved their competence, they told each other.

Dowie Stead was no fool, however, and secretly feared what might not be accomplished; that there might be no consummation to the chase. No blood to dip his fiver in.

"I wonder," he said, "if Blacksmith knows about the telegraph. Gilgandra can telegraph direct to Sydney and so can Merriwa. But there's no telegraph direct between the places where he's most likely to move."

"I hadn't thought of it," said Dud Edmonds.

"He's not as clever as all that," said Toban.

In their night encampments some of then spoke as if the manhunt were a novitiate for the war in South Africa. They were unlike the clerk who gave Jimmie the leaflet on fencing in 1897. Their inheritance—combined—was not in thousands

106

of acres but in hundreds of thousands. Except for Toban, they were Britannically minded.

"What makes me doubtful about South Africa, there are too many fellers dying of disease."

"Righto. Yer got t' risk the disease t' git at the Boer. Righto. They print the list of those who die of disease. But they don't say how many of them've killed a Boer or a bunch of bloody Boers."

Toban said: "There aren't even a few British soldiers 've killed one, let alone a bunch." It gave him satisfaction.

"Yer can't get away from it. Yer look at the lists in the *Herald*. Private Briggs, enteric fever, Private Brown, of wounds, Corporal Jones, enteric fever, Private Smith, enteric fever, Captain Ponce McGillicuddy, enteric fever. The lists are bloody endless. Enteric fever is what they're fighting. The British Empire versus gut-ache. They ought t' put out in front of recruiting places a sign that says *Recruits ought to be told that if they join Her Majesty's Forces they might have to bloody well fight Boers*."

Toban, son of the son of an Irish evictee, spoke as expected.

"It's Britain's war, not ours. Every Australian gets shot or goes under t' fever is a crying waste. We're going to federate. We're going t' be a bloody power in the world. And our world's our world, not Britain's. If it was, why did our fathers and grandfathers come here?"

"Singin' *too-ral, li-ooral, li-addity*," said someone, from an old song about the convicts.

"I can tell yer Father Reynolds, who's of Irish descent all right, but no fanatic, yer all know that, he's just come back from Rome and he tells me Britain's stocks in Europe are so bloody low they wouldn't even buy a pound of butter."

Everyone whistled and groaned to let Toban know that he had been admitted to their number because of his sillabubs and horsemanship and power with liquor, in spite of the colour of his opinion, which was generally anti-monarchist and Papist.

"*Oh Paddy dear, and did yer hear*," they sang at him.

At the end of the hubbub, someone said, "The Boers've got a lot of sympathy, it's true what Toban says. I mean, all they wanted to do was to have their land and keep the black man in his place. Isn't that our policy, here tonight? The Boers wanted to keep the black man in his true naked state. If we hadn't flattered and put clothes on our blacks . . . I mean t' say, our blacks are far more backward than any South African black ever was, and if we hadn't tried to turn ours into Europeans, then—" he coughed, as if worried at reminding Dowie of his grief or duty of grief "—then you know what."

Dowie spoke, with all the authority of his bereaved state, just now suggested. But without rhetoric. They kept Toban for that.

"British authority has been challenged by the Boers. There's been deliberate provocation. An insult to the Queen."

"Pardon me, Dowie. I respect yer right to speak, but I beg to point out the flaws in yer statement." It was Toban again, the great flaw-pointer. "I mean, t' talk about an insult t' the Queen! If an Eskimo in the Ar'tic wrote *bugger the Queen!* on the wall of his igloo, would yer go all the way up there t' shoot him for it? It's nonsense. The Boers are a people like us. They're tough and there wouldn't be any South Africa without them. Just the same as there wouldn't be any Australia if it wasn't for the downtrod of Britain's filthy cities and the victims of tyrannous British eviction."

Again they cheered ironically at Toban's Irish catechisms. "Where from, Toban? Where were people evicted from? What country did that happen in? It's those bloody Catholics again, evicting the poor bloody Protestants!"

"Don't you worry! Our grandparents all had the arse out of their trousers. Out here we live like kings in Australia. Who did that for us—the Queen? My grandfather farmed an acre and a half in Kerry. Now my father runs sheep on twenty thousand acres. And we can afford t' ride out like this, like knights, and hunt . . ."

He began to look solemn, as the other young man had some seconds earlier.

". . . with all respect, Dowie, hunt the killers of girls who nothing can make up for."

Someone said, "Well put!" and the words sank beyond trace into the shadows beneath his jaw.

Dowie Stead let his mouth set in mute lines that could easily be interpreted as grief. Secretly he mastered a compulsion to tell them all to shut up their sombre prognostications. For they nearly all knew what it was to slaver after dark women. Even Toban. And he couldn't blame that on evictions.

In Muswellbrook, Mr Neville told his wife that if he could he would go off after the Blacksmiths unarmed.

"Poor Jimmie!" he was always discovering himself saying.

And always Mrs Neville said, "What do you mean, poor Jimmie?" In a tone that suggested that she might not have married him if she had known of this tendency towards sympathy for killers.

Mrs Neville wept for the obvious things which were all reproduced in one special edition of the *Mail*. The photograph of the Newby family, taken at Christmas time, 1898.

"What a fine solid couple they made," said Mrs Neville of the Newbys. The two murdered girls were marked with a white cross.

"So young, so young," said Mrs Neville.

"But you must remember," said Mr Neville, "that they would have grown considerably since 1898."

"Of course, of course."

There was Miss Graf's firm face, strenuous shoulders and bust.

Mr Neville was no fool. He knew what sickness Jimmie was suffering. Having a true talent for religion, he understood the obsessive spiral, and understood that he himself might have been sent racketing around it if ever he had touched a black woman. The only anodyne, the sole apology for one abomination, becomes a second, and so on.

The *Mail* had printed too a photograph of Mrs Blacksmith, waif-wife in crumpled dress and straggly, bunned hair, squinting at the phosphorus flash. Mr Neville remembered with nausea that he had recommended this sort of marriage to Jimmie, this stupid, cunning and insipid girl. Did Mrs Neville remember that? He hoped to God she did.

Appropriately deaths and burials were numerous in his congregation during the first fortnight of the Blacksmith spree. The Rev. Mr Neville had got beyond the words of the funeral rite and found that total extinction after death and survival in God's sight were both equally hard to disbelieve in.

Likewise he found it only too easy and totally impossible to believe that his Jimmie Blacksmith was at loose killing women.

In Sydney there was a promise of spring, but first, harsh nor'-westers. All Mr Hyberry's customers had colds and Ted Knoller, waiting against the antiseptic wall, sniffled into his scarf with a furled copy of the *Sporting Chronicle* under his armpit.

"Well, they've found two of them," he called across the floor. Once more no one but a reputably deaf spinster was waiting to be served. "The wife and the old man. You'll have to . . . *do the job*, let's say, do the job on them two."

"I wasn't aware they'd come to trial yet," said toffee-nosed Mr Hyberry.

Knoller found the man unbearably discreet and polite. He even had a copy of the Pure Foods Act hung on the wall.

"No, they haven't. But Christ, they were all in it. They're sure to . . . Have yer ever hanged a woman before?"

"No."

"I s'pose it'll present its peculiar problems."

"Indeed it would, Mr Knoller, for the simple reason I'd never hang a woman, even if ordered to do so by the Queen herself."

Behind their father, the slicing boys did not even look up. As if they had been informed beforehand of this possible future falling-out between V R and their father.

"Not even if she's a murderer?" Knoller asked. "I mean, a killer's a killer, it don't make no diff'rence, man or woman."

"It makes all the difference, Mr Knoller. A condemned woman might be carrying another life. However squalid the origins of that life might be . . ."

"Yer mean, she might be in the family way? In a jail?"

"Jails are not all they should be, Mr Knoller."

Mr Knoller was amazed or pretended to be. He pulled the *Sporting Chronicle* from under his arm in a manner that made the butcher fear that he might fall back on it for reference material.

110

"By what yer jest said," Knoller slyly murmured, "you'd be willing to hang a grandmother who was past bearing children. You'd hang her no matter how randy the wardens were."

"I would not hang a grandmother, because I would respect the life she'd already given to the world."

Then Knoller laughed, in a nasty, doubting way. It made him peevish that Hyberry was incorruptible.

The hangman himself found it possible to be lenient with Knoller today. It would be easy enough for anyone to presume that an executioner, given that he was not a monster, would obtain insights into the nature of man and death by all his cool killing.

In fact, all that happened was that Hyberry came to the jail the day before the hanging. Through the Judas window of the condemned cell he surveyed the man, never for more than five minutes. The chief warden already had certain measurements to hand to him as well. Then the gallows were inspected and Mr Hyberry set up and adjusted the rope and tried the trap.

These days it took him up to two hours to arrange matters to the limits of his scruples. Then he went home, unless it was a country hanging, in which case he returned to his hotel. At home he took a double-whisky and went to bed early. In a hotel he might have as many as three whisky-and-sodas in the lounge, reading something such as the *London Illustrated News* until ten o'clock.

The next day he was called at dawn. In a strange numbness he drank his early morning tea, shaved and omitted breakfast.

At six-thirty a cab took him to the prison and he looked over his preparations, though not at his victim. Most of the hour between seven and eight he spent chatting in the Chief Warden's office, where a chaplain would join them.

There was usually a high failure rate in jail chaplains, so that Hyberry found himself frequently explaining to novice chaplains where he himself would stand in relation to priest and warden and physician and statutory witnesses.

The condemned usually behaved well. Hyberry never knew whether it was because the doctor had given them some euphoric drug or because it was easy to die if the hour and

111

moment of death were known. He would never have asked if sedatives were used; it was not his business.

On the scaffold, Hyberry stood at the left-rear corner. The condemned scarcely ever looked at him when they came up onto the platform. Sometimes they were permitted to speak, though were usually dissuaded from it if they were in a God-defying mood.

Then two warders jostled the man gently onto the centre of the trap. Immediately Hyberry came forward, arranged the noose, put a hood over the man's head. Three seconds later he had gone to the lever and tripped it. The clack of the trap did not always drown the incisive click of the neck breaking.

Hyberry had learned no mysteries; he was so deft at the work and so swift that witnesses often wondered why they were necessary.

So there was nothing to tell Knoller, either obscene or revelatory . . . apart from his mistake with the old black man.

But Knoller already knew about that.

11

TWELVE DAYS after Healy's, the Blacksmith brothers were still in forest and had tired of it. It was tricky country. One kept coming on drops of hundreds of feet, perhaps a thousand, and had to scout about for a way down. The descents themselves seemed profitless and unreal. The Blacksmiths had the tedium of ceaselessly outdistancing their pursuit.

They needed the heady sight of hunters; to be made to flee at high speed and in the route of armies.

Fires and long meals soothed them. Sometimes they overslept. Mort spoke, the little he did, of visiting women.

Jimmie believed it was wise of Mort to think of women, and to find Pilbarra camp one night after dark, where he knew a girl called Nancy. Certainly they were reckless, but had come to a point where they needed to be assured of the tangible world of search-parties and towns aghast by the dozen.

So they heedlessly knocked on Nancy's door in Pilbarra. It happened that Nancy's husband was away, but he was a hospitable man anyhow, or if not hospitable, easily frightened.

Both her children were there, a half-caste called Simon and a full-blood called Peter. Nancy took them aside. She had a flat solemn pleasant face. The Blacksmith brothers could hear what she told them.

113

"These two fellers pretty bloody tough, cut yer water off or bloody throat like as not. You git off with yer into bush and catch possum a few hours. Orright? Yer go quiet and if yer go near Constable Harrogate they'll shoot the two of yer and him as well. Off yer go."

Unbuttoning, Mort said, "Who's this Constable Harrogate?"

"All the blacks' camps got a constable, pertect 'em against angry whitefellers. There lot of whites with rifles ridin' up and down the countryside."

Nancy herself was undressing, in a random way. Her kindness to killers—it looked like kindness, anyhow, not fear, made Jimmie's throat stick and caused him to colour and brought tears to his eyes. Her off-hand mercy.

Without warning, Mort fell on her and wept with an alarming loudness, and was soothed into sucking at one of her nipples like a child.

"Yer know what we done?" he asked her, half-choking, his mouth champing at her.

"Yair, yer ripped up some people, didn't yer? Yer ain't goin' t' rip me up though, are yer, Mort?"

Mort howled. Nancy made hushing noises.

Jimmie as well wanted his turn to weep on her, but could not delay the spasm of grief. He fell onto his knees shuddering. It was beyond him to hate the Newbys any more. It was far less than that he felt no victory over them. Their judgments seemed to hang over him still, of their own strength.

So Jimmie was still the victim. The obviousness of the fact bent him to the ground abjectly, as Healy himself had been bent.

Then, as Mort still sweated towards satisfying his mothering Nancy, Jimmie lay inert, his mouth open. He could neither move nor imagine himself ever moving again. It would take someone to come armed and demanding surrender to undo his paralysis.

Someone came armed and demanding surrender. Mullett had at last heard of the murders and gone to the police. While drunk, Mort had mentioned Pilbarra to Mullett's woman.

114

A small force of police and citizens, headed by Farrell, had met Dowie Stead's party, who were moving west again. In another case such a reference to one village might not have brought forth a large concentration of force. But it was the pattern of the Blacksmith chase that hundreds of men would ride hundreds of miles on a rumour.

Therefore Farrell had been able to collect constables and volunteers as he went.

At eleven that night, Nancy left the brothers drowsing and went to her burlap doorway: the last look of the night, to call her children home if they were waiting in the dark for a sign from her.

What she saw was a bonfire in the centre of the camp where police and armed volunteers were guarding the men-folk who had been flushed from their shanties at the south end of the camp. This gambit looked as if it had been in pro-gress for some time, the blaze, the herded men, all achieved in near silence.

When the Blacksmith brothers knew they took their rifles and cartridges. Everything was so quiet; it was one of those nights when you can almost hear the frost turning to crytal on the earth.

"Don' leave yer food," Nancy begged them, for they looked like men about to sprint. "Don' leave yer bloody blankets. C'mon, Mort, don' be a bastard. It'll all make me look damm silly."

Like a pressured husband, Mort began to gather his blankets and load of food.

"Yer can't bloody fly with a mountain in yer beak," Jimmie told him.

Mort shook his honest head and put them down again.

"Yer can't, Mort. I bin fair."

But Jimmie Blacksmith, holding the burlap ajar with his rifle, was already pointing a direction. They slipped north-wards from the door, towards the dark fringe of the camp. Jimmie Blacksmith was sick with fear of death.

Someone took a glimpse at them from behind burlap. They were an event, likely to be brought to a killing peak by fusillades from the camp perimeter within ten seconds or so. Jimmie's throat was dry deep down into his guts, and he was certain of his own death. Too frightened to move or stand still, he remembered the presage of women's blood, and then the virgin Christ barbarically used; but could not find a mode in which he should prepare for dying.

He scarcely thought of Mort's feelings. There was terror in them too, but a fatalism too. Dulcie's sad white man had bred most of the fatalism out of Jimmie, who now sweated on that account.

Anyone else who saw Jimmie Blacksmith and Mort would have said they were moving with great craft on the dark side of the shanties on the north of the camp. They did not look like men filled with complex dread.

Then, as often happens in places charged with fear, an unexplainable event occurred.

A young white—it was Toban—stepped in front of them. He peered and was out of place, blinded perhaps by watching the bonfire. In his hands was a shotgun.

Mort was so close to him that all he had to do was lower his rifle and shoot the white man in the stomach. Toban fell backwards cawing like a woman. Within a second the earth was slippery with his blood.

About them people were running, there was the hooting of the women and the baritone orders of white men. But Toban, silent now, and Jimmie and Mort did not move. Toban grunted, not much more than a man trying to settle in bed. His eyes were open and he seemed very much at rest.

Then, all his old moralities jangled by the events at Healy's, Mort re-loaded. Jimmie, seeing in it Mort's loss of innocence, was indecently pleased.

"Jesus and Mary!" said Toban. "Don't do that. I might live."

But Mort shore his head apart with a shot.

The brothers still stood, physically feeling the tides of sound in which they had made their new killing; but a comforting killing, this time, a hunter brought down.

It had all taken seven or eight seconds.

Without a word both sprinted east on rising ground. There were bullets at random from their left but the far uglier noise of hoofs to their right. By mere yards they evaded horsemen. After half a mile they hid their rifles and climbed into a

116

peppermint tree, a familiar smell, hinting at childhood, and painful initiation by stone, and Methodism.

They lay flat-out along the limbs, warily regaining breath. Survival had made them drunk, the canny air they drew delighted them.

Both of them were bare-footed. Shoes, food, blankets were all back at Nancy's place. Nancy would have to explain them. People like Farrell would be very hard on Nancy.

"You and yer bloody women," Jimmie whispered.

And on his branch Mort was still elated and laughed beneath his breath. He did not remember and never would, that his rigor with Toban was an infection from outside. He seemed to be content that it had arisen from an antique code and was aligned with frequent placation of spirits and rare tribal face-to-face warring. Besides, Toban was a man. That itself seemed a wonderful renewal to Mort.

Five whites and a constable galloped by, found the ground ahead too heavily bouldered, turned confusedly right, and halted. The policeman and two followers got down from their saddles and went off, crouching, towards the boulders. Meanwhile the other three dismounted at greater leisure, ready to shoot any Blacksmith who might be flushed from cover.

Not being shot dead or jumped on from behind, the policeman and two volunteers returned to their horses. Then the party rode south.

The Blacksmith brothers climbed down to earth and went up the spur behind the boulders. They loped at their ease, back again in country where the horse was futile. Such terrain meant something to them now. But it was cold. Jimmie was aware of the precarious warmth of his body moving through absorbent veils of cold.

They were above two thousand feet when they stopped. Below them they could see a line of campfires, though they could not afford one for themselves. Tomorrow, men would rise up from the cinders and climb after them. Jimmie did not suspect, though, that that was the reason why Mort bedded down on the cold, spine-niggling earth with such compliance.

On this, the dry and hardy side of the mountains, they had

117

to part and look for shallow water on rock ledges.

Jimmie found some where there would have been a water-fall in wet weather. But all the rain that had drenched them on the way to Mulletts had failed to crest the Divide and fall here.

The water had a slight vegetable stink to it, but was delightfully chilled.

He drank and went back to meet Mort, whose luck had probably been similar.

It was sick-grey quarter-light and the harsh myrtle-trees watched him with the remote quizzicality of witnesses.

When he got back to the place where they had slept he found that Mort was standing agog for the sound of Farrell's wakening army and had painted his face white with white clay. This in the morning! As if he were resigned to dying.

It made Jimmie peevish. He came snorting up.

"What's this bullshit?"

Mort continued in his listening stance. He explained in his own language.

"Our enemies have found us. We wanted white ones to kill. Soon there will be white ones, tribe on tribe. We shall make a mighty killing."

"So'll bloody they," Jimmie said.

"We shall die in courage. They will chatter about the courage of Tullam man."

Jimmie could almost have given in, thinking again of all the weary savageries he might have to do to imply a meaning in what had already been done.

"But we got t' show we ain't jest women-killers."

"They know 'bout that. Yer fought the Newby boys fair."

It was a bad time for candour, but Jimmie couldn't help himself. It made him testy: Mort should have been able to sort the truth about what had happened at Newby's from what he beheld at Healy's. It seemed pig-headed of Mort not to have understood and accepted the full toll of Jimmie's murders.

"It weren't the Newby boys. It weren't old Newby."

"Christ, what yer tellin' me?"

"What I'm sayin'. It wasn't old Newby and his sons."

The ghost face peered at him. Mort rose.

118

"It was bloody old Mrs Newby and the girls and that bloody schoolie."

"Yer fuckin' devil-man," said Mort after some seconds.

"I'm yer brother and I got bloody mad and . . . It'd happen to anyone. C'mon. We gotter git some food and blankets." He snorted because the mute face did not move. "I got t' show 'em I aren't jest a woman-killer."

"They know yer fuckin' devil-man."

"I'm yer brother. Yer shot a woman yerself."

"That was acc'dental."

"All mine was bloody acc'dental."

"Yer better git away from me, devil-man. Yer better go away."

"Orright. Yer better stay here and pertend t' be Ned Kelly. They'll shoot yer into mince."

"Orright. I don't care. I'll show 'em we ain't all woman-killers."

"Orright. Yer kin go t' hell."

They gazed at each other for twenty seconds. Across their silence came a clear white shout from beneath them. Suddenly Jimmie could see that, under the heavy white clay, Mort was holding tears. He was only a boy, and now his brother had his soul.

Therefore Mr Jimmie Blacksmith started off on the jog. A minute later he heard Mort behind him. Slantwise, across his face, Mort had made four furrows with his fingers in the clay matt.

As the morning turned blue and the birds began to sing he even began to seem a little reconciled to living. But he said, about mid-morning, "If yer married Mungara none of this would of happened. Now yer kin see why Tullam takes Mungara."

"Horseshit," said savage Mr Jimmie Blacksmith.

To make false tracks that morning they rode some cows they found high up. Mort laughed again, rolling about on the loose pelt of his milker. Half a dozen times he must have come within an inch of pitching off, which did something for his buoyancy and made him loose and agile with hysteria.

A calf loped behind, moon-eyed and confused at this strange usage of its mother.

By midday they came on shallow, clear water. They did not resist the main line of the Divide, which took them north-east towards—once more—the cluttered forests leading to the Barrington Tops.

It seemed they had made an honest escape and were a little heady with it, even Mort, after the morning's vicious revelation. As Jimmie marched he suffered minor but lasting unease about the mad bounty of Mort's love and loyalty.

He had not resolved this disquiet when at three in the afternoon they came to a smoking little home in a clearing of rich tropic grass. A white horse, whose belly scarcely cleared it, cropped away, the fattest horse you could possibly see, his underjaw bald and spiky, a horse kept out of sentiment and beyond his twentieth year.

There were neat sections of cross-cut red box in the wood-heap, and a washing line, where a woman's nightdress caught the sun coming down steeply but full over the top of the cedar and tall blue messmates of the forest.

The Blacksmith brothers circled the house. It was well-kept. It could have been a logger's. It could as likely have been a miser's. For Jimmie had heard of misers in this part of the country, where the defiles were said to run with alluvial gold and the jungly ridges hid prodigal veins of quartz. Old fossickers, it was said, kept maps in their head and nuggets in gunnysacks under the floor.

But all Mort thought of was the nightdress.

"Let's get on," he kept mumbling. "No more bloody women."

Jimmie walked on in his circle behind the first veil of forest. He could not have explained what he was waiting for. It was some sort of mandate to remove every unjust man, every miser. He was a tender-hearted murderer who needed to feel that he was priest and judge. If this man, with his house-pride and pot-bellied horse, were an unjust man, he would show it by the way he answered and so be fair and obligatory game.

If on the other hand Jimmie now closed out his count of killings, he sensed, he would be left with a long contemplation of the deaths he had wrought.

"Go t'nother place," Mort spat, half turning back into the

120

woods all grey and blue with afternoon, no comfort in them, damp earth.

They had not eaten for a day.

Jimmie waited without hope for the sense of mission to come to him, by which he could with assurance pounce forward into the sight of men. His great fear was suddenly that when the high moment of encounter came, how could you depend on a white to be ugly or to blunder?

Then an old thick man came out of the house, stood at the door and called strongly to someone inside, something loud but conversational. He was a block of a man. He picked up his axe and began to split the sections of box-tree with a hint of enjoyment.

The Blacksmith brothers unaccountably (they had lost full self-control after Healy's) stepped forward together and came at him across the sunlit quarter of his yard.

Very soon he saw them and stood up straight with the axe held across his chest. Indeed he was old, seventy years or more, but no part of him seemed yet to have begun to sag. His nose was imperial, his mouth tucked into a wry corner at one end; giant veins stood out on the insides of his elbows, and his hands were large beyond the limits of belief: rampaging veins ran across intricate scars, creases. An atlas of great tree-fellings.

Jimmie already began to believe that his anxieties had been prophetic.

"Yer the Blacksmith boys, aren't yer?" the old man stated.

"Yair."

"Yer bin killin' all them poor women."

"We ain't killin' no more women," said Mort. "Yer kin tell that t' the p'lice."

"We shot a man last night," Jimmie contributed.

"God forgive the two of yer!"

The old man bent and began to beat the wood from around a knot.

When that was done he stood straight up again—no clutching of the spine. He looked at them. His great nose was the nose of a prophet or general.

"I got a wife sick in bed. Aged sixty-five years. Yer goin' t' kill her?"

He was over seventy years but believed in forcing issues. He was not afraid. Unless he were immediately shot he would undermine them. But he refused to take on the victim's manner. He was immensely older than they were and vastly cunning.

"We got no food at all. We need some food and blankets." Jimmie Blacksmith, who had kept an army in the saddle, felt intimidated and immediately qualified, "Two blankets would do O.K. And some beef and tea. A billy too."

"Why should I feed yer? Yer unclean."

"Listen, take us in the house."

"I forgot. Yer a bloody specialist on indoor work."

"Take us in, mister," Mort pleaded.

Inside, the warm breath of the open hearth drew them. It was all one room. There was a brass-knobbed bed in the corner and a small oval-faced old woman in it. From the centre pole of the roof hung a meat-safe. Jimmie glanced at the woman and opened the safe door. There were two lumps of corned beef rolled and skewered. One was half eaten. Jimmie took the other.

"Want a burlap," he said.

"Yer'll find one about," the old man advised him. "These are the Blacksmith boys, mother, but they aren't goin' t' kill us. God won't allow it."

His decree ran hypnotically between the woman and his visitors.

Jimmie was furious with the wrong sort of fury, the anger of a subordinate. He savaged the tins above the mantel but left enough for a meal or two in each.

Apologetically, Mort examined the old man's rifle, which was wired together at stock and linstock and probably past use. Then he prodded some traps with his foot.

When the food was packed, tossed without system, rice on beef on water biscuit, Jimmie approached the bed.

"Yer can't take our blankets. It might be September but we're still gittin' cold nights up here. We only jest got enough."

"We ain't got any."

"We earned ours."

"Let 'em take the blankets, Dad," the old lady whispered

122

again and again at the hem of her counterpane. "Let 'em take the blankets." It was like a private prayer.

"Orright," the old man said. "Shoot us now jest as well as take our warmth."

"Yer got a bloody fire!" Jimmie roared, pointing to it.

"Of course we got a fire. This country's too damp. . . ."

With his way of forcing every demand to a peak of challenge, it was a wonder the old man hadn't been shot fifty years past. In other ways, it was a wonder he wasn't an archbishop or premier.

Jimmie snatched up a shawl and a loose blanket.

"We gotter have these ones," he told the old man. It was close to a plea, because Jimmie felt weak with the thought of this newer injustice: that the old man should occur now and suck their fibre, when he might have occurred earlier, barring the way to Newby's, saving a man from madness.

12

In Dubbo, at the same time, Mrs Blacksmith was dismissed from custody. There was no indictment against her bunned hair, her crushed green dress. She passed into another capture.

Two Sisters of Mercy took her away in a closed carriage. There was a jolly Irish one who put her finger on the baby's chin.

"Yer dear little dove," she said, "yer young t' be after leaving prison. None of my family ever managed it so young. They'd be jealous. Yes they would, pretty baby."

She produced a brown cord with two little felt squares attached, one of them a picture of Virgin and Child. She arranged the cord about the child's neck so that one square lay on its chest, the other fell down its back.

Tears were in Gilda's eyes. She knew that as a mother she should resist such encroachments. But her tears had no authority and her large straw hat put them in deep shadow.

After Toban's funeral, three of Dowie's party made their case for going home and went. It was not for fear of the Blacksmiths. Everyone knew, by noon on the day after Toban's death, that the Blacksmiths could not now be found by any amount of dedicated riding.

One of the young men wanted to enlist, the other two had

124

their fathers' acres to attend to, and—in every town—letters of paternal complaint waited on them calling them home.

In October, the Blacksmith brothers dared cross the Divide and come down to the western slopes, circling Tamworth at night and north-west then, towards the towns of the plains, Wee Waa, Gunnedah. Insensate travel for its own sake, innocent of scheme, its direction betrayed by their need to ransack.

They travelled at night. Two days of rain they spent cosy on top of a provident farmer's high hay storage beneath a chattering tin roof.

Deep in interstices between hay-bales, in the dusty corridors mined through last season's fodder, rats or tired black snakes moved. Mort would sit up, listen for a few seconds, become reassured and lie down again on his spread blanket. He wore only his trousers; it was steamy beneath the iron roof. He was full of alarm of things—grain-rats, for an example—that would once never have worried him.

In the small hours of a Friday they came on a lit-up hut whose owner, a neat-suited little man, had come out to his doorstep, spying on the stars and approving that they could all be seen while, by the light over his shoulder, he took the cardboard stiffeners from his hat.

The Blacksmiths spied on him in turn and Jimmie envied the day's business he would do in Tamworth.

The brothers spent the rest of Friday there.

Once inside, Mort slept, but Jimmie found a corner of newspapers. The top was a *Herald* of September 30, 1900, the bottom a *Mail* of May 1, 1899. Jimmie opened them at random in the dawn light. What he looked for were items that proved his own sharp reality yet at the same time did not raise in him any ambiguities of feeling. He did not want to be further confused.

First he found a reference of Toban's death. It satisfied him to know the boy's name.

Frank Toban became the latest victim of the black desperadoes as the result of an unfortunate mistake. Police and volunteers, acting on information, had surrounded the aboriginal reserve at Pilbarra. Mr Toban, a member of Mr Dowie Stead's party, was asked to go from one station on the reserve perimeter to another. He was unfortunate enough to have met the Blacksmiths amongst the shanties on the northern edge of Pilbarra. It seemed that, after shooting Mr Toban in the stomach and head, the brothers escaped through the very hole in the defence which Mr Toban had been on his way to cover.

This further exhibition of barbarity . . .

But Jimmie skipped the moralizing.

Yet he could not make himself forgo seeing the earliest reports of those eons-old killings at Newby's. He rummaged until he found the appropriate editions. Though he could not read well and did not want to read them head-on he brushed his eyes up and down them and could sense a crystalline indignation that made his nape prickle. Finding a far too appropriate *Mail* edition, he saw a photograph of the Newbys' house, substantial, ugly. He felt nauseated and forced the copy deep into the 1899 end of the pile.

"Fuck up the old bastard's system!" he muttered.

Then he found that Jackie Smolders had been sentenced to death.

Yet it was touching to see this old man in the dock, a grizzled elder of his race, painfully respectful of those about him and of court procedure. It made even more incomprehensible the outrages he found it in him to commit at the Newby homestead at Wallah in July. . . .

The twelve sturdy Dubbo men and true who made up the jury withdrew, but returned after ten minutes with a verdict of guilty as to the charge of the murders of Mrs Newby and Miss Vera Newby, and accessory to the murders of Miss Mary Newby and Miss Petra Graf.

Asked if he wanted to say anything, the old man rose and spoke as follows: "I only wanted to give Jimmie his initiation tooth [a ritual tooth to remind a black of his tribal obligations —Ed.] to let him know he shouldn't have married a white girl. Mr Newby wouldn't give us food so we went to argue with Mrs Newby. We never expected for a second we'd kill them. Jimmie was a good worker [he added, rather irrelevantly] and I ain't afraid of dying because I earned hanging with what I done [sic].

I never done nothing [sic] like this before. You would

think it would take up a good while to make up your mind to kill someone and then to kill them. I'm just an igorant [sic] black man but take my word for it, it only takes a second."

Poor Jackie Smolders giving the people of Dubbo an honest warning against the suddenness of homicidal fury. A few of them might live to be in need of it.

Mrs Gilda Blacksmith gave evidence on the first day of the trial.

She is a thin girl who looks more fourteen than eighteen. She displays a considerable compunction for the time she spent with her black husband and says she was often afraid.

They didn't say what of, that was the point. And *black husband* was unfair, he thought. The white seed might have been the bad seed.

She said that she and James Blacksmith had been respectably married before a Methodist minister and due witnesses in Wallah in May. In July a child was born to her, somewhat before its time, at the Newbys' homestead. . . .

Jimmie trembled: intrusion dressed up as Newby charity. As for Gilda, he felt the pity which a man can easily mistake for love. She existed less for Jimmie than did, say, Mrs Healy, and he could not hate her, seeing through the news report her transparent cunning, her bankrupt ambition: to escape charity and be acknowledged as her own voice.

Five days later, a number of Blacksmith's relatives had arrived and two hovels were built beside the Blacksmiths' small bungalow. She said she had felt afraid from that minute. Asked if she received indecent propositions from any black man other than her husband, she replied no, but that they had drunk a lot and that her husband had to put much expense towards keeping them there.

Without warning, newsprint in disarray all about him, Jimmy understood that he had a copious love in him and had not spent it. He would die with his head full (he thought of it as a headful) of unspent love. The waste of life he had already made certain of. The truest crime remaining to him to commit was the waste of love. It should be bequeathed, as land is.

He began to compose a message to leave here for Gilda

and the cook's child. But then people are not always happy to receive inheritances. Perhaps he could say or beg that the child should not be treated in terms of the murders its father . . . its father (let it stand! he thought) had done.

And he could say that Jackie Smolders was a gentle man, liable to fright.

But then he imagined the press reducing the importance of his *will of love* to something inane and comic, as they had reduced Jackie Smolders with their *"sic"*. *"Sic"*, Jimmy felt sure, was a term of superior mockery.

In the New South Wales Legislative Assembly, he noticed, there had been a second reading of the Attorney-General's Bill of Outlawry of the Blacksmith Brothers.

The journal was at pains to instruct citizens on their rights under the bill.

This bill will increase penalties against those harbouring the fugitives, provide a reward of £5,000 for their capture, and cancel all the Blacksmiths' rights under common law and the law of the State. They can be shot on sight, or—if captured as the result of surrender—be put to death, it seems, without question, by any citizen using any means of execution.

Jimmie Blacksmith was, in fact, cheered by the rigor of official opinion, by the absolute nature of outlawry. He decided he had best get some sleep. But before he drowsed off, two other minor items of news attracted his eye.

One in the exact, high-toned *Herald*.

The date of the execution of Jackie Smolders, condemned to death in connection with the Wallah massacre of the past August, has not been stated, and informed observers say that it may be a policy matter to postpone the execution until the capture and trial of the Blacksmith brothers. An officer of the Chief-Secretary's department has stated that it would be considered inappropriate for the State to conduct executions in relation to so emotional a matter as the Wallah massacre at a moment so close to the great event of Federation.

In the more sentimental *Mail*:

Mr Toban was a member of Dowie Stead's band of comrades, who all intended to enlist for South Africa once the Blacksmith killers had been tracked down. Therefore it can be said that the cowardly bullets of James and Morton

Blacksmith have deprived the Queen of a fine soldier.
Beneath it were published the Boer War casualties:
Private Ian Manners, N.S.W. Mounted Rifles, enteric fever.
Lieut. B. Griffith, N.S.W. Light Cavalry, enteric fever.
Sergeant L. Peters, N.S.W. Mounted Rifles, of wounds.
Private Edwin Clarke, N.S.W. Horse Artillery, enteric fever.

Mort was better sleeping by day. Sleeping by night, he did things that worried Jimmie. He would throw off his blankets and walk a few yards in a daze and plump down again to sleep without covers, on bare ground.

But, a fierce mover, he ate up distance whenever they travelled. Jimmie, night and distance he challenged with the width of his stride.

"The stain is on the inner eye," he would sometimes mutter in Mungindi. It was part of a cautionary saying:

> *Woman's blood cleaves to a man.*
> *If he wash his eyes over and over in Marooka,*
> *His outer eye does not see it again,*
> *But the stain is on the inner eye.*

A hunter sighted them near Murrurundi as they turned back to the mountains, and they were chased by a constable and twelve citizens into intractable gorge country to the north, a land that suited and awed them.

Friday was the best day for looting, the day country people went to town. Jimmie survived by a centimetre a Friday afternoon presumption that a farmhouse before them was empty. For days after, he kept feeling on the right side of his neck the cold breath of the passing bullet.

Onto tablelands of sheep farmers, but still October and the first days of November could have nights too chilly for them. The north had bristled, the south was too open, and Mr Jimmie Blacksmith wondered if he could withstand the echoes in the deep woods and high divide near Merriwa. Due east from where they now stood the timberlands went down to the coast, Jimmie knew. There was good cover all the way down to the pleasant estuary town of Taree, a town which

Mrs Neville had always claimed exceedingly to like.

First they were in high clean vertical forests, little under-growth, little debris on the ground. The unearthly place worried Mort. Jimmie hoped it would give onto rain-forest.

Soon it did; cluttered, homelier, creeping with insect industry. Staghorns grew on the trees and tipped crystal water into their sleeping faces. Quick wakeful brown snakes were out in their new skins. The bush-spiders were large but wary. All this somehow made it a more humane country.

The fires they made gave piquant, moist smoke that stung the eyes and made good tea.

About them, sown with little timber hamlets, spinney on spinney stretched broader than England.

They found an empty selector's house. Someone had gone bankrupt up here in the wet forest. He had left seven bed frames, a few old copies of the *Herald* and the *Freeman's Journal* and one black-and-white coral snake in methylated spirits. It was easy to feel sad at these few relics of hope, though Jimmie remembered immediately his own depreda-tions against far more prosperous hopes.

Here, with stub of pencil and on the margins of old news-papers, he left parting messages for Dulcie, Jackie, Gilda, the child. The letters might never be found, and that allowed him to write more freely than he could have dared do in more frequented places. It was mad, but allowed him to say gener-ous things to Gilda.

Dowie Stead had become more indecisive with all this riding. He had even forgotten his relief at being excused from taking Miss Graf's high hand in marriage. The faces of the slaughtered had become remote. Miss Graf awaited resurrection in Gilgandra cemetery. Her agony was folded away now, like washed, rolled bandages that once wrapped screaming wounds.

Dud Edmonds had begun to suggest a return to normal business. Soon the shearing season would begin. The world or the wilderness would consume the Blacksmiths in the end; they would fall down a gorge or be torn by random bullets of farmers.

But Dowie shook his head. He felt he had become a figure

of sentiment and that the sentiment must be maintained. He spoke of "being in at the kill". His father, besides, kept sending bank-drafts, as if their share in a black whore compelled him to it.

Sometimes Dud's conversation would niggle at Dowie, hint at the inanity of the chase and the shadiness of Miss Graf's memory.

"Yer going t' join the Masons now, Dowie?" Dud knew that Miss Graf had made it a condition of betrothal that Dowie should not join a lodge. "Yer old enough t' join now, Dowie."

"Petra wasn't strong on it. She said it was like black magic. She said it was like a corroboree."

"I don't see how she could say that. She might've meant *Boaz* and all that. But there's nothing the matter with *Boaz*. It's all based on the Bible and Knights Templars."

"Knights Templars?"

"Crusaders. They were the beginnings of the whole Freemason business. And the blokes who built the pyramids."

"I wonder if they've gone down to the coast? Round places like Port Macquarie, Taree. The Blacksmiths, I mean."

"I know a family in Taree, Dowie. Two nice daughters. Yer can't live like a monk for the rest of yer life."

Dowie uttered an ambivalent grunt. "Well," he said, "the Blacksmiths aren't going to try to live like monks. As poor bloody Toban found out."

"Poor bloody Toban. Yer know, I don't think he really meant all that Irish business and running down the Queen. I wouldn't mind betting he would've turned Mason."

"Never."

"Yair, I tell yer. In every community yer got them. The ones who join in to serve—like yer own father—and the ones who join to *be* served. Toban would've joined to be served."

"That's a bloody awful thing to say about a dead friend."

"Death doesn't alter facts."

It seemed clear that Dud was aiming at throwing question on Petra Graf's image, that Toban was merely the first step.

"Shut up, Dud. Yer bloody indecent."

"Listen, Dowie, there's a lot of bullshit talked about death."

"Jest wait till you've had a dose of it."

131

"Come off it, Dowie. We both know you didn't want to marry that Graf girl."

"Shut up, Dud."

"Look, I've stuck with yer . . ."

"Don't make a song and dance about it."

"At least I ought t' be allowed t' talk honestly. I'm just as shatoff with the whole business as you are."

"Righto! Say what yer bloody like."

"Listen, Dowie, yer know yer'd jest as soon not git yoked with that high-hat schoolie."

Dowie felt naked. His face ached with shame. For some seconds, he felt he was about to assent.

Then something unfortunate happened. Dud had not really wished to speak honestly, not with penetrating honesty. He was, in fact, the sort of man whom society could depend on not to let the cat out. So that he now went grey with alarm and dropped to his knees, hanging his head.

"I'm sorry, Dowie. I oughtn't to say that. Yer can punish me if yer want."

At least it fruitfully occurred to Dowie how lush with gesture and eccentricity people could be, the quietest, safest people. He himself had his hand half-way to Dud's shoulder; but then needed to go beyond the firelight to cry. A man did not cry, as he did not perform a natural function, within a fire's ambience.

He wept for not having wept for Miss Graf. He wept for his father. What's the matter with me that I can't feel grief in its proper place?

If he gave up the chase, he feared, people would spot it in him: that he didn't feel the correct, the *ordained* things.

Dud waited up for a while, then arranged his blankets, sighed, and went to sleep.

The Blacksmiths were hale. Around Gunnedah and on the tablelands they had eaten only the best of mutton, slaughtering at will on the big sheep farms. Therefore the November damp of rain-forest did not penetrate them. If the high sun touched wet cloth, steam rose in the warm air. The winter of their bloody doings was over and they might live for ever in the coastal valleys.

132

Yet they would not have chosen to. To deliver themselves from the ceaseless trees, they again willed deliberate crises on themselves.

One midday they crossed a track with wheelmarks deep in it and came to an open slope where two buildings stood. One was a schoolhouse, *Tambourine Public School 1891*, it claimed in black paint. Behind its window was a burr of talk or rote learning.

Below it was a school residence with children's clothes on a cord across its veranda, declaring some unknown woman. The woman came out after they had waited half an hour, felt the clothes, winced and went indoors again empty-handed. She was young but older than they. Her parted hair, unpinned, obscured her face, but Jimmie's special sight picked out a brown eye, a pale nose.

After his long abstinence, he feared so much that he might want to kill her that the impulse actually arose. As he fought it, it seemed to grow with strength borrowed from his own marrow and guts.

Both brothers fell asleep and were awoken by the afternoon thunder. It was mid-afternoon, and Jimmie was peevish, sleeping too long and from fear that he might ravage the woman.

"Schoolteachers spreadin' bloody lies," he said, half-conscious, and felt vindicated when his senses cleared and he found that the teacher was busy spreading one now.

The children were chanting:

> *Australia is*
> *The smallest continent,*
> *The largest island,*
> *And dearest land of all.*

"That ain't his bus'ness," Jimmie said. "*Dearest land of all.* That's got fuck-all to do with school-teachin'."

"What's it bloody matter?" Mort asked. "Every kid in school gits taught that."

"Fuckin' dearest land of all!"

"What yer goin' t' do, shoot him for it?"

But the incantation over, children marched out, broke ranks.

133

A boy got another down in the long grass and punched him square in the face three times, then let him up. Even the after-school loitering was clipped. The children had to ride home to help with the afternoon milking.

They were all gone in five minutes, kicking old bareback nags up the cart-track. Then the teacher came in his vest, rolled-up sleeves, watch-chain and Wellingtons, his coat over his arm. He was short, but with a rangy country gait. He had glasses, a Society of Friends beard; and looked aggressively content.

When he vanished into the residence they heard him calling out greetings to a child, and, from further inside the house, a girl's light voice telling him with a little dissatisfaction of something domestic.

Then he came out again to chop wood. The Blacksmiths made for him.

They were only yards away when he saw them. He looked up at them through strong lenses that magnified the eyes beyond them. These eyes, Jimmie could tell, were trustful in the sense that they had had experience of human rancour yet still could not break themselves of some habit of credence.

"I know who you two are," he told them. "God, you've travelled fast."

Jimmie could not allow people like him to establish their intent. He raised his Enfield and sighted it on the schoolmaster's heart. For two seconds he clenched his eyes shut and then fired. The bullet went well wide of the teacher. Those two blind seconds had cheated or saved Jimmie.

"Jesus!" the teacher muttered and sat down on his chopping block.

The thin girl who had been sighted earlier came onto the veranda and began to scream.

"It's all right, darling," the teacher called. "We spotted a rabbit. You go inside. I'll be in in a moment."

The girl's large eyes were not reassured. She remained where she was and raked her hair from her forehead so that she should not fail to see any further pot-shooting.

"C'mon, Jimmie," Mort said. He was afraid for the witnessing lady.

134

"No."

"C'mon!"

There was silence, set against the small-talk of forest, of falling twigs and chattering birds. The schoolteacher began to speak but gave up and drew his hand down the length of his spiky hair from the back to the forehead. A gesture of conciliation.

Then he said, "If you two gentlemen are in any doubt as to whether to kill us, just let me tell you my wife's sick and I don't have much insurance." He struck his fist three times on the knee of his trousers. "And we're *both* bloody innocent."

"Yer got any flour, bacon?" Mort asked.

"Oh yair, enough of that." He shrugged and looked up at them, his lips quivering beyond control. "You don't have to think you *must* kill me. You let an old man live up in Barrington Tops."

"Soon as we turned our backs, yer'd be off to the p'lice," Jimmie said. "It was a schoolie did for Ned Kelly."

"You're welcome to take my horse. I'm twenty-two miles from a police station. A walk like that would take me two days. Look, I know I can reason with you, because you aren't mad, either of you."

After a second of looking up from beneath his eyebrows, and looking always more and more blameless without trying, after an instant of licking his long sad lips, he laughed sharply and in considerable fright, and stood up.

The Blacksmiths could see that he understood—perhaps from the classroom—the ways control shifted from one to another and that he suspected it might somehow pass to him; that, at least, his family would not be hewn or shot.

"Let me show you something you'd enjoy. It's in the *Bulletin*."

Mort followed, dangling his arms, and Jimmie came too, though much more creakily, his rifle at the port. There was one of those near-comic crushes—somehow implying the parlous state of Jimmie's command—at the doorway, where the schoolmaster halted for the sake of frankness.

"By the way, you aren't going to believe me if I say I've got no arms in the house. In fact, I've got a bonzer Martini Henry carbine. My father-in-law gave it to me. I've been intending to clean it—I haven't touched it for a year. It was a wedding present. Everyone said it was a funny wedding present. Someone said it was to keep the cow-cockies away from my wife. I haven't got any ammunition for it."

They went on then, into the kitchen. The teacher chattered on, the wife watched out of her vast witnessing eyes.

Meanwhile Jimmie felt desperate. He was letting consequences pile up against him by letting them live. Yet he had no passion for this woman's blood.

He screamed for the teacher to shut up and hit him on the jaw. The woman shrieked at the blow. Her husband began to weep silently in a detached way, in a way that did not diminish him.

"A schoolie did for Ned Kelly," Jimmie diagnosed. "I don't want no schoolie to do fer me."

"Yer got any liquor?" Mort asked dismally, as if the terms they were negotiating had shrunk to that. "There won't be anythin' more bad happen t' yer, missus," he muttered at the woman while the teacher went fumbling for rum in the kitchen cupboard. The teacher passed a flask to Mort without interest and held out his arm to receive his wife.

"It's all right," the teacher said, whether instructing Jimmie or comforting his wife no one could tell. "If they were going to kill us, I'd tell you so that you could pray. My wife is religious."

"We're Methodist," Mort stupidly said. "We not goin' t' kill yer, missus."

The headmaster blinked. Gobbets of tear were spiked on his lashes. He began to look around him.

"Where's that copy of the *Bulletin*, dear?" He found it slung across a dumb-waiter. "Here, look at this."

It was a caricature of two plump aborigines camped in a forest setting, feeding police bloodhounds with legs of mutton. One of the two aborigines was telling a satiated police-dog, "Go back to yer boss an' tell 'im yer ain't seen nothing!" Both natives were smiling, and the one not bribing the bloodhounds was reading a newspaper which bannered the news: *Blacksmith Brothers still at large after two months.*

"What's it say?" said Mort, after Jimmie had read the thing a second sombre time.

Jimmie explained as drily as he could manage. He was unwilling to confess being touched. But once the bones of the joke were stated, Mort propped himself up with Mrs Healy's lady-companion's rifle and bent over with laughter, and then Jimmie himself conceded, and the headmaster smiled.

It was preposterously more than a joke. The pen-and-ink man had restored the Blacksmiths to the comic realm, an area which, they thought instinctively, everyone had closed to them. It gave them leave from the corroding business of being incubi; absolved them from the bogy role. At once Jimmie saw the remote potentiality of becoming a figure of myth in this first breaking of the monumental visage of appal the press had so far turned towards their fumbling homicide and talent for flight.

And the teacher knew all this.

"There've been three thousand men out looking for you two, you know," he told them.

"Three thousand!" Mort whispered. In a sparse country, Mort was impressed by the immensity of thousands.

As the wife told Mort where the groceries were kept, Jimmie remembered the passage in the *Herald* about saving Jackie Smolders' hanging until the Blacksmiths had been taken. The idea of a hostage, of someone who could be bargained for Jackie Smolders, came to him.

He knew how unlikely the concept was. But here they had been treated with a sort of respect, been given room to speak in their true selves. It was all so simple: they wanted to go on being seen as the two gay fugitives of the caricature. And this teacher was a man to whom they could speak of their crimes in level, wholesome, even comic terms.

Jimmie could not have explained all this. But for taking a white with them there was one word, which the force of his understanding pushed up his throat.

"Hostage," he said, and everyone became silent.

"I couldn't keep up with you two. I'd hold you up. I've got respiratory trouble."

Besides which, Jimmie knew, there was a great risk of the prisoner becoming master. Some of the blindness that goes with falling in love forced Jimmie's decision. Mort's eyes also shone. He wanted company.

137

"We wouldn't hurt him, missus," he said in actual apology. "Three thousan' sure t' catch us in the end. Then he kin come home."

"Git yerself some blankets and ground sheet!" Jimmie told the man.

Instead, the schoolteacher was caressing and soothing his wife and began to argue against the nonsense of taking him. But, being no fool, he began to see that they were answering one of the imperatives of their history and were fixed.

Soon his wife was fussing about, packing his things as if he were going for a train journey. It was all very insane. "Take the double blankets," she said. "Keep warm but not too warm. It's a dangerous time of year. And wear your rough-work boots. What about Wellingtons?"

"It's too hard trekking in Wellingtons. Have you seen my *Palgrave*?"

"How many pairs of socks? And don't forget to keep the flannel round your chest."

She was meanwhile seeping tears all the time.

They left well before dusk, so that she could start for a neighbour's place before dark. She stayed on the veranda, spilling tears and chewing her bottom lip.

It was like a dream, this fantastic insistence on a hostage, and had no more logic than a dream. They found that the schoolteacher's name was McCreadie. Now they intended to show McCreadie the daily virtue of their fear and strenuous survival. He had short breath, however.

"I warned you," he said.

It rained and the schoolteacher's asthma became louder in the slowly dripping, still forest. Towards one o'clock in the morning they halted.

McCreadie sat against a trunk, assuring Mort he was not as ill as he sounded.

"The secret," he grunted, "is to get rid of the entire load of air before breathing in again. Most asthmatics take short, quick breaths, but that only makes things worse. A person must never panic, or think that each time he breathes out is the last."

"Panic?" Mort asked.

"Do your bundle," McCreadie explained.

Mort understood that that was how McCreadie had won,

by giving things time, by passing around the latest edition of the *Bulletin*.

Spreading a groundsheet, Jimmie saw Mort gathering kindling wood.

"No fire," Jimmie said, "They'll be lookin' fer fires."

"Who'll be fuckin' lookin'? The schoolie needs a cup."

"Don't be such a bloody ole lubra. He's here fer us. We're not here fer bloody him."

"Mort wants one too."

"Fuckin' ole women's church turn-out."

But he drank some when it had been brewed. Then McCreadie put his glasses away in his jacket, his eyes with the blunt look of the acutely short-sighted, and began slowly rolling himself in his blankets.

"No school tomorrow," he wheezed, before going soundly asleep.

The McCreadie-Blacksmith connection was initiated by Jimmie in the hope of finding a genial self-reflection in McCreadie. But people are never passive mirrors.

Jimmie became quickly disenchanted with the teacher who seemed to be receiving confessions from Mort, or perhaps even conspiring with him. Suddenly McCreadie began to see little comedy in two men evading three thousand, and became fixed like Mort on the fact of Jimmie having axed women.

Mr Jimmie Blacksmith felt as cheated as a man who marries a bitter woman. It was clear that the teacher would emasculate and sunder them; and that he intended it.

Meanwhile Jimmie wanted to be blunt and vicious with McCreadie, in the manner of a Healy or a Farrell; but harshness like that did not transfer well to the teacher, who could not be appropriately frightened or angered.

On a clear damp morning, for example, he fetched water from a mountain sink in sandstone, a fed pool with sweet little crayfish in the soft abrasions of sandstone which covered the bottom. He filled a can, and rose to see McCreadie gathering wood in the undergrowth ten yards away, his suit collar turned up and his elf-shaped ears pink as if it were mid-winter.

He went straight to McCreadie. As often before when Jimmie had confronted the teacher, Mort materialized from the forest to watch, to see after McCreadie's welfare.

"When I went t' work fer farmers, fer farmers like Newby," Jimmie said, "they was always afraid I was goin' t' turn their prop'ty into a blacks' camp. They always said a *filthy* blacks' camp. It looks as if yer aren't keepin' yerself very clean, Mr Schoolteacher, and *I* don't want my place turned into a filthy whites' camp."

Then he poured the can of water over McCreadie's head. It washed the glasses off the short-sighted eyes, turned the beard to a thin goatish tassel of hair and flooded the good cloth of his shoulders.

But the act worked no magic for Jimmie. McCreadie's wet pink ears and beard and all made a flat joke. Of course, Jimmie Blacksmith understood, the reasons why it was a flat joke were the same reasons that made vengeance a yawning lie.

How Mort would once have laughed, the young Mort. The Mort he had become groaned his intolerance across the space between them.

A quick shiver ran through McCreadie, but he did not move.

"Yer stupid bastard, Jimmie!" Mort called, passionately, a genuine opponent.

"I'll tell you," said the schoolmaster, "if I get one of my chest inflammations . . ."

"Go an' fill up the can," said Jimmie. "That'll help keep yer warm."

"Why don't yer go an' fill it yerself?" Mort suggested. "Yer the stupid bastard that spilt it."

"What d'yer think I am, the bloody schoolie's servant? Yair, yer'd like me t' go, so yer kin tell him how yer never cut up any women an' yer a nice abo off a mission."

"Well, I never cut up any women."

"Jest shot one in the chest. But that don't count, I s'pose. Christ, they ought t' have yer fightin' the Boers."

Without warning, McCreadie, a gobbet of water still on his nose-tip, let out his classroom roar.

"Be quiet!"

The arguing brothers were jolted more than they cared to be.

McCreadie said severely, "If you stand there comparing evils, you won't stop till you've shot each other through the heart. You ought to know that no one does a murder unless he wants to."

Jimmie Blacksmith morbidly hoped McCreadie meant that, for it would weaken him with Mort, who believed now that people could stumble into the act of killing.

"Yer kin hurt people by acc'dent," Mort said.

"Oh yes," the teacher conceded. "But you harmed the people you harmed because you chose to go to them ready to harm them, with the arms to do it."

Mort put on a sulky face, as if he were hurt to be lumped with his brother, the axe-murderer, and disappointed by Mc-Creadie's poor opinon of him.

Once more the thought of shooting McCreadie came to Jimmie, but dismayed him. The startling thing was that a bullet could not hurt McCreadie on the plane on which Jimmie hoped to hurt. Something so endowed with energy and the grace of the Lord as a bullet from Birmingham could not prevail.

"I'll go and get the water," said McCreadie at last.

He went away in the maladroit amble Jimmie Blacksmith had become accustomed to seeing. A stiff, sick-man's walk, anyone could see.

Yet he had such hopes for, such need of McCreadie. It was not to be thought of, letting him go.

Not only in his butcher's shop was Mr Hyberry considered wide open for scrutiny. As Grand Master of his Balmain lodge he must endure a Master who, far from being a night foreman of a marshalling yard, was a State Member of Parliament and an industrialist.

This man was delighted as a child with all the lines of influence he controlled, and enjoyed flexing them in public to show people that they really existed.

Grand Master Hyberry was always surprised by the man's blunt line of approach.

"Hah!" he'd say secretively, whenever he met Hyberry, "tell me, Grand Master, did you ever go to sea?"

They might talk health, weather and the vague politics which are all a politician can afford to speak with strangers. But it always returned to, "Tell me, Grand Master, did you ever go to sea?"

The parliamentarian had been to sea. His father had owned small clippers and once he himself had signed on for the Sydney-Valparaiso-London run.

Mr Hyberry always said no, he regretted he had never been fortunate enough to go to sea. Then the politician would actually begin to talk of knots, of knots and seizings; unmangeable, iced-up knots off Patagonia.

It was not as subtle even as Knoller, but the purpose was the same. They wanted to find out that he was privately a monster with a profound lust for his task.

Hyberry refused to tell them how he had had a sober maternal uncle, a devoted man who, fallen to arthritis, merely wanted to hand on an onus of public duty to someone who would carry it with dispassion.

In the early hours of a November morning, however, Mr Hyberry, sleepless in his high-prowed marital bed, could not be dispassionate. The loud-mouth politician had told him—in confidence!—at lodge the evening before that the Premier had put down Hyberry's name for an M.B.E. on a preparatory list of nominations for royal honours. The list was to mark the new year and the new federation.

"But he can't now, Wallace, yer understand. Not till those Blacksmiths have got caught. If they git shot, good-oh, all above board! But if yer have to hang 'em, what with the public interest in the case, it'll look like yer gitting a reward for stringing them up. Never mind, in a year or two . . ."

Mr Hyberry wanted a royal honour, humbly knew it to be his due. He thought it was unfair that whether he got one or not depended not only on the normal vagaries of politics but on who committed murder and when, on when they were captured and tried, and on the intensity with which their murders struck the public mind.

"I mean t' say," the politician had said, "it'll be hard enough choosing a time to hang 'em. Everyone'll be in such a high frame of mind with all this federation nonsense. Hangin' and things to do with it'll be a little bit out of place."

They would probably give the M.B.E. he coveted to a senior sewage engineer. For sewage was less contingent than crime and punishment.

13

A ND NOW McCreadie became a habit. He would hold his
breath and take the risk of beginning to speak of
bloodlust and murder.

"I can understand your being angry," he would say in the
midst of a night silence. "Oh, I can imagine it, Jimmie. I
mean, settlers still talked about *marauding blacks*. Only ten
years ago they did. But how many whites really ever got
killed by aborigines? No one knows. I bet it wasn't more than
four or five thousand. If that. Then, you might ask, how
many aborigines did the whites kill? The answer is a quarter
of a million. Two hundred and seventy thousand have gone.
I can understand your being angry."

Jimmie secretly loved to hear these admissions. They were
the luxuries he kept McCreadie for.

Then McCreadie and Mort would argue about *their* killings. Perhaps it should have been hard for Jimmie Blacksmith
to listen. It was easy; because crimes like the Wallah massacre
made the criminal, him, Jimmie, feel remote, a phantasm; and
his terror of unreality, of hell, of demon-harbouring, could
be soothed by this sort of debate.

Mort could be depended on to debate, and McCreadie
could be depended on to mention everything, even—in the
end—Healy's baby.

"Yair," Mort said, "but Jimmie's wife says she's goin' t'

have Jimmie's piccanin'. When it gits itself born it ain't' his but some white bastard's."

"But don't you believe your totem . . . your animal spirit . . . that's what makes children come?"

"How yer know all that?"

"A man called Andrew Lang. He writes about it."

"I'd teach him t' write if I got hold of him." Mort was frightened and angry about Andrew Lang's writing. God knew what secrecies of his heritage were written down for whites to read. "Not white childs get born that way. Only black. Black mother, black husban'. It's pricks do the work all the rest of the time."

For the first time Jimmie saw that Mort was aware yet unaware that they were only half-brothers. You were brothers or not brothers. The two governing elements were Dulcie and Emu-Wren. *Half-brother* was a white genealogical nicety.

McCreadie listened with respect, polishing his nose and worrying runny eyes with a handkerchief, his breath grinding up and down his throat.

Because of this weakness of the wind they needed to scout ahead, one waiting with McCreadie for his breathing to improve.

"Inhale, exhale," he would groan, doing his strangled breathing exercises. "It's a bad time of year. The air is full of dust and pollen and animal hair. I can't even ride a horse in October or November without getting sick."

The Blacksmith brothers argued sullenly with each other, about cooking and brewing tea and fetching things. They clung to McCreadie as mediator, yet maintained to his amusement the fiction that he was a hostage. For the fiction's sake, they lost five miles every day of the week.

Yet they were not moving at random. They were travelling in what should prove to be an unexpected easterly direction, down the valley escarpments to the sea. When they slaughtered cattle here, farmers presumed it the work of timber-fellers, who were notorious gatherers of free meat. Jimmie's tactic was to go south and cross the Manning River by boat and continue on into the hills above Port Stephens.

Heedlessly, he mentioned Port Stephens in front of the

144

teacher, talked of hiding away in one of the American timber ships that came there for the cedar. It was a soothing proposition; America was as good a hope as any to invoke.

McCreadie was thinning. The high colour of his ears was bad health, not weather-blains. Against the spitting fire and within the dome-like, hollow noise of rain in timber, the rasp of McCreadie's patient strangulation could be easily heard.

"You better let me go," he'd murmur. "I wasn't raised to do this sort of thing."

But both brothers needed a third party, could not imagine speaking to each other without McCreadie about. Also, McCreadie filled and diverted their day. From dawn they would bicker about the man, arrange concessions to him, grumbling about poor mileages, choosing camp sites, granite ledges with overhangs.

McCreadie peered at all their quarrels as if about to intervene like a polite guest and say they should not go to trouble for him. But he said nothing; his eyes simply descended through plane after plane of wistfulness and he gave small, tight, unavailing coughs that did not dent the surface of his asphyxia.

At one time they had to let him rest for two whole days. They each let him have their second blanket, and wrapped up by Mort he slept with a look of intense obedience on his face.

"Sleeps like a bloody nigger, that feller," Jimmie remarked and laughed paternally.

Suddenly the weather got drier, the sun took on an Advent ferocity as if to dry out the fervour of Christians in that hemisphere. They were pleased to be in cool places, ragged country that cast shadows. The summer skirling of cicadas began. They smiled about the hubbub, sadly. For that insect rant was at the heart of their first memories; their first prey on summer mornings about 1886.

They were near the coast road now, going very slowly yet, luckily, in an unlikely corner of the coastal hills. McCreadie was not better. His big eyes knew that he must soon prevent them from sucking at his substance.

"I know all this country," he told the brothers. "I was raised just down the hill, about twenty miles down, near Croki." He pointed to the summit of the hills just to their left. "There's something up there I want to show you. A big place of stones. Holy stones. Magic ones. Shaped like a womb. For initiation, you understand. For when they circumcised the boys." McCreadie made weary cutting motions. "The whole of the Manning River tribes used to use it."

Jimmie Blacksmith was suddenly jealous for black secrets himself. He asked how McCreadie knew so much. McCreadie again invoked the name of Andrew Lang.

That sort of stunt put Jimmie in a fury. All scholarship came down to Newby refusing groceries. Andrew Lang had not written Newby into a generous state of mind. Andrew Lang was therefore just a prying bastard.

"We don' want t' go t' a place like that!" Mort said quickly, because there was a strange pull in the suggestion.

"I was coming up this way one day," McCreadie chattered on, "when I was about ten. An old black met me and said if I went up there that day I'd get my water cut off. I think they used to use it as recently as that."

"Why do we want t' go buggerin' round a place like that?" McCreadie's wide eyes flitted about for a reason.

"There's no one to visit it any more," was the best he could manage. "They've got all the poor blacks herded together down at Purfleet."

He didn't dare say too much. He had found the place potent and believed it might act potently on the Blacksmiths.

Mort was talking urgently in the secret language, while Jimmie hawked and pretended not to be touched.

What Mort was suddenly proposing was that they should face the cherished centre of another tribe, test their justice and magical immunity against foreign spirits. They would find out all at once if they were cursed. Mort was suddenly keen on instantly knowing.

Mort taunted his brother in the nasal, falling tones of Mungindi. Jimmie listened and made mouths, coughing the fright and dryness out of his throat.

"Orright!" Jimmie kept roaring. "Orright!"

At the end of patience he asked McCreadie, "How bloody far t' this place?"

"A mile. Straight up the scarp. You can see the sea from up there."

"Orright. If yer both got that much wind . . ."

The dread of his assent and of the sight of the sea thoroughly parched Jimmie out. For he expected a high, reeling, vertiginous place.

Their native awe of where they were going was coloured by the residue of H. J. Neville's Christianity. So they were raiders and outdarers and adjurers but also pilgrims, bearers of onus, seekers for justification, desirers of exorcism.

"Rest, please!" McCreadie had to keep demanding beneath his rattling breath.

At one pause Mort painted his face. One must use every subterfuge in the heart place of another race, one must caulk one's flesh. Jimmie himself would have liked to do it.

"Fuckin' stupid boong," was all he could say, for he could not claim the same native rights as Mort, and resented it.

When McCreadie said they would see it in half a mile, remarkable things began to occur.

Mort took a branch and flayed his body with it and then, strangely, Jimmie's back. Not a genuine flagellation, a mock one, like the flagellation of monks. Jimmie, whose face McCreadie could not see, tolerated it.

It lasted perhaps a minute, then Mort ran ahead with the branch, laid it on the ground and began to kick dust over it.

McCreadie did not understand, except that it was some rite of deception or diversion of spirits.

Soon after they stepped out of shadow onto a wide abutment falling away on the east to the Blacksmiths' first, remote sighting of sea, a mere inverted triangle of hazy blue between coastal hills.

The place itself was terrible enough, compelling. Molars of rock eight feet tall had been used to outline the womb and between the monoliths ran smaller stones white-grey. It was spacious and holy here. Even if it were only clean magic that had been practised, it had been practised long, with such hope, such memory and dedication. Here black boyhood was fashioned to the purposes of tribe and marriage, hunting and kinship, confirmed in a special and delicate vision of the world.

Now the vision and memory lay truncated and blurred in

147

places like Purfleet. So it was a sad place, it waited for restitution.

The entrance of the womb was on the north where the platform met a face of black-stratified rock, looking in the manner of *The Moonstone*, thought McCreadie like a god from whom a diamond eye has been stolen.

Mort and Jimmie had dumped their gear at the south end and began to skirt the stones, Mort with his hands out—implying goodwill—and chanting a broad drooping chant. What he sang was:

> *Strangers yet well-intended we have come,*
> *Wary of strangers' totems,*
> *Fugitives who have seen all the bad omens of blood*
> *And need the mercy of foreign people,*
> *Warmth, song and food.*
> *Moving forms of men wanting their souls returned to them.*
> *There is nothing we wish to destroy,*
> *Being already under threat from wronged spirits.*

It was contradictory to use poor subterfuges such as face-paint yet then to chant such admissions. But even Mort had lost some of the black protocol. Jimmie sang nothing and was afraid. Gasping McCreadie could see the fear and perhaps confusion. Mr Jimmie Blacksmith, mighty terrorizer, lost beyond repair somewhere between the Lord God of Hosts and the shrunken cosmogony of his people. Mort Blacksmith, however, still had his nearly intact black soul. Surely his brother saw it, McCreadie hoped. In his fever, and head light from lack of breath, he believed the womb a violent place. Like magnet to magnet it snatched up Mort's mind. It left Jimmie unpolarized though uneasy. *And surely Jimmie saw it!*

I have separated them, McCreadie thought, staggering, sweating, eager for breath. Or assured their separation. No small thing. No small thing.

But the state of the secret place disturbed him. Many of the large stones had been toppled, the small glaucous ones uprooted and heaved in every direction by picnickers; by exhibitionizing young men of the Manning valley. By young

148

men in love whose tongues were no more fitted to speak love than hoofs are, but whose hands were big enough to hurl large rocks in celebration.

There were inanities written too on the slabs. There were bottles broken and rebroken to small pieces. Mort's feet, summoned by awe, trod without harm on the amber grit.

Both great stones marking the womb-mouth were in place. On the left hand one a message was rasped deeply by knife. "CENTRAL TAREE—MANNING RIVER CHAMPIONS 1897". Then, in charcoal—"TAREE—NORTH COAST CHAMPIONS 1898. DEFEATED PORT MACQUARIE 27-2."

McCreadie felt ashamed. Such a threadbare response to a ritual gate, a stone-age basilica; not like Stonehenge, millenia-abandoned and a prey to tourists and the graffiti of corporals from Aldershot. A *used* place, this. There were men in Purfleet who knew what the uses were.

Had the footballers from Taree, heady with their twenty-five-point margin, been so incurious as not to stand back and ask what the pattern was and who had made it?

McCreadie felt the heat of tears on his lids. He fingered one of the desecrations.

"That's awful," he said. "That's bloody awful."

On the right portal was, "MCCAFFERY SLEPT HERE." "SO DID BAINSHAW." "CLIVE LOVES IVY FROM THIS DATE, 21.2.93." "CLIVE'S GOING WITH A BLACK GIN. WATCH OUT IVY, 16.11.94." "CROKI RUGBY PREMIERS 1898."

McCreadie said, "This is dreadful. This is too bloody dreadful for words."

The nursery refrain: *Build it up with iron bars, iron bars* ran through his head.

"We must build it up again," he said, listening to himself with amazement, knowing himself to be agnostic as Zola or Marx could want. "God will forgive us if we build it up."

Jimmie began arguing, on practical grounds. It would take them all day, he said. But it was no use being reasonable with Mort and McCreadie.

They went on with their survey. A desecrated aisle opened out spaciously, and to one side of the inner wall stood a prow of stone in tilted layers. Perhaps the fertilized ovum, McCreadie surmised, on the womb-wall. Did the elders know as much anatomy as that? It was a natural stone, not man-hauled, and its sea-facing front had lateral clefts. Scattered around it were fragments of small stone that looked as if fashioned. The Blacksmiths knew what they were, *tjuringa* stones, each the external capsule of someone's soul, some black man initiated ten or fifty or a hundred years past.

And those who picnicked here had been thorough. The *tjuringa* had been fished from the clefted rock in dozens or perhaps hundreds, small smooth wedges, a few intact, others snapped across the middle, others ground with perverse injury to smaller, irreparable pieces. Soft coastal *tjuringa*, loose-grained as the souls they held, too much yield in them, no ferocious, tight-texture. Far too like the men whose calyx they had been. Far too like the yielding loose-grained men of Purfleet, Burnt Bridge, Verona, Pilbarra, Brentwood.

And here the history of mean death and lust for booze and acquiescence to the white phallus, gun, and sequestration and all the malaise of black squalor, here it was, legible in the fracture lines of soft stones.

Sensing all this, Mort howled from the heart of his own torment and fell down on his knees and elbows. Jimmie crouched and as if from curiosity but with massive secret fear picked up some of the more cleanly broken stones and pieced them together, keeping on his face a handyman frown.

Close to him the teacher's eager breath grated like a pump. And after a time, the teacher could be seen heaving some grey stones that were meant to fill in the ritual outline.

It had become easy for him to believe, his mind all cross-eyed for lack of air, that if the Taree footballers had not fallen to celebrating their skill on the consecrated stones of another race, there would have been no killing at the Newbys'. It seemed to him almost a principle of law, viable in a courtroom. He would state it when the Blacksmiths were taken.

They scavenged around, not doing much that was helpful. At last Jimmie came up.

"It ain't no use," he told McCreadie. "It's buggered an' no help fer it."

The sun was low and their sweat felt cool. As volatile as bay rum to fevered McCreadie.

"You must leave Mort, Jimmie. You can see that."

"Mort's been in on all I done."

"He wounded a woman, but she's getting better."

"He shot Toban. I need Mort. Mort needs me."

"Would you say so, Jimmie? Would you?"

Mort was at that moment raising a shaft of stone and dismally watching the insects writhe where it had lain.

"You ought to bugger off, Jimmie, and give him a chance. You ought to leave us."

"Why in hell?"

"The boy isn't really your brother. He's an aborigine, Jimmie. Not like you. There's too much Christian in you, Jimmie, and it'll only bugger him up. Like it's buggered you."

Jimmie should have been angry, but shrugged.

"I'll ask him."

"Don't ask him. He'll stay with you because he's an aborigine, and loyalty's in it." McCreadie shivered from the intensity of debate. "You have to just bugger off. At night."

He half turned to look at his brother. Oblivious amongst other men's totem ruins, Mort had his head tilted. It was a wedge-shaped family head, rather lean. Jackie Smolders had had it, Mort had it. Jimmie owned a squarer white face but with a splayed black nose in the midst of it. A dead give-away. The sort of thing that, Newby had assured him, could never be bred out of his line.

"I'm taking it for granted," McCreadie said, "that you love Mort."

Mr Jimmie Blacksmith said softly, "Yer better wrap yerself in a blanket, mister, and jest shut up."

But of course he knew it was all true; it was all inspired truth.

Dowie and Dud, recovered from that clumsy impasse by the campfire, decided that they might go down to the cool hotels of Taree and, bathed, make decisions there about their future pursuit of the Blacksmiths.

The valley restored Dowie. It was wide and rich and river-dominated. The sun came out of the sea and made a long and profuse haul to the Divide. The river was stippled with the mouths of surfacing perch, was Mississippi-wide and full of vistas and luxuriant islands of silt.

They bathed and had a late breakfast over the Sydney and Brisbane papers. The news was all Federation, and articles on the constitution and how the High Court would settle quarrels between States and the Federal Government. A biography of the Governor-General, projection of the Queen's sacred majesty, made Dowie feel meritoriously bored.

Kruger had fled into Portuguese East Africa. Lord Roberts had declared the Transvaal annexed, but a special correspondent doubted that the war would end:

A member of a captured Boer commando told me that his people can and will go on fighting for years in a countryside they know better than any British soldier could be expected to. Because of their small numbers and mobility, they would not be subject to the deadly diseases that attend the transfer of masses of troops in an unaccustomed climate.

"Your people think the possession of towns is everything," he told me.

There was a lesson there. Small numbers and mobility in a countryside they know. The Blacksmiths.

Joseph Chamberlain had declared the new Australian constitution a highly advanced model of parliamentary and monarchic democracy. There was an editorial praising Chamberlain for the praise.

One felt a certain accord with these high sentiments after a ride down the velvet Manning slopes and a good bath.

The *Manning Times* wanted to interview him. Did he think the Blacksmiths were in the valley? He said that they were always in the places they were not expected to be. They were so slippery that it might be the best thing to look out for them in the direction they were least surmised to travel.

Then Dowie and Dud talked politics in the bar. Dowie was a little disappointed with the conversation. He would have liked to think, as the beer worked on him, that with his good looks and laudible purpose he appeared to the rich town of Taree as a personification of the new Australia.

But Dud was more that, draining beer through lean lips and giving inexact and minimizing opinions of all the new century's hopes.

"See, the parlerment's supposed to meet in Melbourne till a capital city is chosen, not less than a hundred miles from Sydney. Well, what'll it be? Gulgong? Adelong? Wagga? Dubbo? Gilgandra? Can yer imagine a country with a capital city called Wagga? Not on yer life. Make us a bloody laughing stock."

There was a certain meanness of spirit in Dud, mistrustful of any magnificence that distant statesmen gratuitously predicted for young countries and centuries.

Later in the day, Dowie was surprised to hear that, merely on his own quoted word, a citizens' committee had been formed to arrange patrols of the town and the river.

It was embarrassing.

14

Mr McCreadie, the comforter, was now fevered beyond comfort, and rode on Mort's back or Jimmie's.

It seemed that he grew clear of mind for a few seconds each quarter of an hour or so. Then he would drag on his porter's throat and there was sharpness and clarity as he asked, "Are you still here, Jimmie Blacksmith? After all this time, Jimmie?"

He nattered a great deal, rhymes and declamation, the sort of thing people go in for in delirium.

> *Yea, welcome March* [he declaimed] *and though I*
>   *die ere June,*
> *Yet for the hope of life I give thee praise,*
> *Striving to swell the burden of the tune,*
> *That even now I hear thy brown birds raise. . . .*

He said it in gusts, his chest crammed against Jimmie's shoulder-blades or Mort's.

In this way they carried him for an entire day. All the time they hoped that in spite of their own laxity the necessary decisions would somehow form and take them from the flank.

The night was cool. Mort swathed the teacher up heavily and sat over him. Each time McCreadie spoke, Jimmie gave a soft dismal snort, as if the presence or illness of the teacher were a genuine pain to him. Mort felt Jimmie had little right to make such a noise, and suggested he get a meal ready.

And Jimmie obeyed without a word, eating at a great pace once the food was prepared, strips of corned beef fried a little too well, therefore hard and fibrous. Jimmie sat there, gnawing the meat with a hurried patience, a humility.

Finished, he threw the fat on the fire and watched it flare.

"We have t' do somethink with the schoolie," he muttered. "Yair?"

"We ought t' put him on a farmer's veranda, knock on the door like, an' run like buggery."

"Jest leave the poor bugger?"

"They c'd git him doctored."

Mort went back to the bundled teacher. Another inspection filled him with doubt. "D'yer think so?"

"Er course. A doctor'll have him right in no time."

To Mort's jangled emotions it seemed an unfairness to have to deliver someone as intimate to them as McCreadie up to a doctor whose name they did not know.

"T'night?"

"Er course, t'night."

"If we git caught . . ."

"Yer orright, Mort. Yer never killed a soul. I'll tell 'em."

"Eh, what's this?" Mort picked up a valedictory element in the statement.

"Fer Chris' sake."

Carrying their proper loads (they tied them onto their belts or around their chests), they shared McCreadie for about a quarter of a mile at a time. The woods became sparser and there were lamps twenty miles away, across the river, that they could see, and ones nearby, one mile or three. The night was a royal blue but distances were unscannable.

Jimmie was about to flit into this soft temperate night. He delayed under the hallucination that he might be able to confess to Mort that he was unconsolable for corrupting him. But it had all happened under such sudden obscure furies that though he loved Mort, whose laughter he had ended, he could not believe himself a devil; but he was sorry.

He could not hint that Port Macquarie might be another

good port for foreign vessels. Mort did not need his guidance on travel. He needed simple deliverance. He needed what the State of New South Wales had had for three months —the disappearance of Jimmie Blacksmith. Whether boats came to the coast from hell, California or China was futile talk.

It was not much after nine when Jimmie laid McCreadie down in his tracks and scouted ahead down the track.

Swaddled and hooded, McCreadie lay where Mort waited, for it was his turn to carry. The fervor of cicadas drilled in the ear. The red-hot lust of the brute earth to flesh itself out with voice and bug-eyes and dry twiggy locomotion had brought them up out of the pores in soil. After a dark glutinous incubation, they now had a short season to rant, to burr and shriek notches in the night's smoothest edge.

For the first time Mort felt hostile to them. In his nineteen years he had never thought of being hostile or otherwise. The concept of any genuine alienation from earth or beast had not entered his head.

And where was Jimmie?

The schoolteacher's breathing could have been mistaken for a slow stroke of a cross-cut saw. At the peak of every intake of breath he managed a few irrelevant mutterings.

"The symbolist bastards . . . Too bloody hard to write poetry now . . . Too hard . . . The articles on Malarmé . . . I wish I'd never heard the bugger's name . . . Malarmé . . . It's a long way to Paris . . . Not unpatriotic . . . But a long way to Paris."

And where was Jimmie? Mort jumped over the teacher and sprinted down the purple night. Wild grass as high as a harvest tripped him up and he grazed his belly on the corner stump of a dairy-farmer's fence.

"Jimmie!" he yelled.

Loping for the river, Jimmie heard him but kept to his duty.

Mort begged the richly pastured night. "Jimmie, Jimmie." Gone with all his excuses for doing monstrous things. Excuses Mort had rarely listened to with respect, now regretting this neglect. It was kin duty to listen to excuses. What other bastard would?

"Mourning my kinsman," he sang to himself. But the chant choked on itself. Not that he failed to see how Jimmie's vanishing had taken an onus from him. And there was love in the absence of Jimmie, Mort had no doubt of it.

Jimmie had left him native. Mort did not see that—he would not be Mort and native if he could. All he could sense was the love and Jimmie's death.

Being native, he swallowed grief down into his veins, where the festivals of mourning could proceed in the tides of his blood. Once a shearer's cook in Cowra had said, more or less, that the primitive nomad did not live inside an idyll but within practicalities. Even the canons of marriage and kinship and magic rites were—in primitive terms—mere practicalities.

Eons of fierce self-discipline were written into Mort's guts. He knew therefore that the practicality which was McCreadie lay choking up the track a little. Within two minutes he was back with the schoolteacher.

He carried McCreadie in his arms, putting him to ground to open and close the yowling country gates. In this way he acted the reliable cross-country traveller. That was how they had all travelled—Jackie, Gilda, Jimmie—on the very first night of their flight.

The roll of blankets loosened and one dropped. He did not stop, but hitched McCreadie higher, as one hitches a large child.

"Wives of schoolteachers," McCreadie said. "In rural areas . . . Rural areas—Christ! . . . Three shillings allowance a week. For taking sewing lessons . . . Three shillings! . . . I call that . . . generous."

If Mort had understood that this rural schoolteacher he was hauling had been clever enough to drive Jimmie away, he might not have sweated so much for him. Or might have felt obliged not to sweat so much for him, out of respect for Jimmie.

"Forty per cent vote," McCreadie said. "They ask the people . . . They ask the people what they want . . . They ask them . . . Nationhood or six bloody . . . colonies? The smallest continent . . . The largest island . . . And dearest land . . . They ask the sods . . . Forty per cent bother to vote . . . Forty per cent . . . Still on the frontier . . . Why bother t' vote? . . .

157

As long as the boundary fence holds? . . . Why bother? . . . Forty per cent . . . They don't know . . . They don't want to know."

Now they were close enough for Mort to see the slanting roof of the farm. The farm dogs were already barking, and McCreadie made croakings of alarm in his throat, a schoolroom reproach which, in his condition, sounded so much like a death-rattle that Mort stopped to shake him out of it.

Through the home paddock gate, he went perhaps ten yards and put McCreadie down. The bundle seemed as small as are the bundled bodies of the dead. How had they managed to make this good man small and sick? It was hard for Mort to understand that some men's bodies might put up physical barriers against fifteen-mile-a-day marches in rain forests. It was easier to believe that they—his brother and he—had passed on some malignancy.

The farmhouse door opened, it was so full of light, and the bald, blinking farmer was edged with gold.

"Who's that?"

Mort called out in the nakedness of his blacks'-camp vowels.

"Got Mr McCreadie here, the schoolteacher from out at Tambourine."

The door flew shut. The gold snapped off, and behind the window, the lamps were being turned down low. A gun barrel nosed at net curtain. There was the awful farting roar of a bullet and Mort felt dirt fly near his ankles. Inside the house, two women at least were weeping, expecting depredations.

"I've got three sons," the farmer lied at the top of his voice. "They've all got rifles. Yer better put Mr McCreadie down and bugger orf."

There was another shot, and Mort felt in the soles of his feet the thud of it in the deep moist soil.

"Watch out," he yelled. "Yer might hit Mr McCreadie."

"Then clear orf and leave him there."

"Orright."

The dogs were standing in their leashes, half-throttled to be at him. He went politely, re-latching the home gate. He hated to leave McCreadie to the heavy doctorings that whites went in for.

Hard-headedly, without too much sentiment, he recognized all the portents that went to prove bedevilment: the red ankles of brother and maternal uncle on the first night; the red omen likewise on the breast of Mrs Healy's tough lady; the harm that had jumped without his willing it from his hand to Toban's body; the infestation of Mr McCreadie.

Now he had nothing to do but act upon the fact of his history of bad magic.

He ran north, coming to one of those steep timber roads where there are usually traffic, schoolchildren, bullock-teams dragging great stalks of cedar on braked tray waggons, rich farmers with timber concessions as vast as Flanders. Here he slicked his face white and slept without blankets, hunched belly-on towards his token fire of twigs and old eucalyptus leaves.

In the dawn he woke as a farmer rode past on a huge snorting grey. The man reined to one side and squinted at him through the trees; then seemed to demand tip-toes and speed of his horse, who was too prestigious a hulk, too quantitative and well-fed, a horse of substance, to give either.

So early in the morning the farmer had been wearing, Mort noticed, butterfly collar and suit, and did not seem to be armed.

The morning was dull and cool for late November. Since a cold death would change nothing, he wrapped a burlap sack around his shoulders and prayed for his daily bread and to be delivered from temptation.

At last the man in the butterfly collar came back frowning with three others from behind the underbrush on the far margin of the track. All four had rifles and seemed intent on taking him unawares.

Aware, he smiled for a second and waited. Thunder rolled familiarly, without ill intent, along the top of the hills.

They conferred then, very close together. They had hats and dolorous moustaches. Two of them wore old collarless shirts and the fourth a deep-blue flannel vest, with a new narrow-brimmed, full-crowned hat, the type popular with rich men and politicians.

Someone, Mort heard, was having trouble with a bolt handle. Then, in an instant, they were dispersed and hidden.

They were not such fools. They were acquainted with the landscape and now implacably concealed.

High to his right the thunder nestled itself down amongst its daily hills.

Then he was shocked by two terrible impacts from his left that lifted him almost to his knees; low, keenly placed, exact bullets, but cancelled a second later by two like impacts from the right.

He lay as Healy or a rabbit, forehead down, worried for breath, appalled more by the force than the pain.

Life, he sensed, was cast in certain jagged rhythms and there was some sort of lasting merit if a person gave himself up willingly to them.

Meanwhile, the man in the suit arrived above him. Empowered by the New South Wales Government's Act of Outlawry to do anything he wished, he lowered the rifle muzzle close to Mort's left eye. Jagged rhythms. Yet it seemed that all his soul jumped with an electric thrill to that threatened eyeball and bled softly from it.

The black man was dead. The farmer desisted from blowing his face apart, remembering that reward might depend on easy identification.

Eight hours later Dowie and Dud rode up to the barn where Mort's body lay on a bench, a blanket up to its neck, its face washed black again. He had been bled in the cowshed and dogs scented the stain of his historic blood on the earth floor, and cattle lowered their slow snouts. The photographer from Taree was packing his equipment into a dray, but recognized the young men and asked for the favour of an on-the-scene photograph.

Such is the power of the press, even of the *Manning Times*, to magnify and consecrate that Dowie and Dud felt fulfilled, justified in the epiphany of phosphorus flash. As a result they stayed at the farmhouse that night, celebrating with the farmer his giant-killing.

One week later, their pictures all appeared in the *Mail*, high-chinned, craning faces, their rifles propped on the floor, their big hands on the barrels that looked like sceptres.

At lodge, Wallace Hyberry's political friend had news. He had spoken to the Premier about the butcher's royal honour, and the Premier had hinted that if Jimmie Blacksmith were to be shot down as his brother had been, there would be no reason why Mr Hyberry should not be honoured in the January 1902 list.

The politician expected to be thanked for this inside news, so Mr Hyberry thanked him; but was sleepless all night again with the implications.

The public—and the Premier, one of the public's highest forms of self-expression—were interested in protecting themselves from killers. But executioners were mistrusted, especially if they had the sweet honour of exacting a publicly-stated, publicly-felt vengeance.

Seven years before, a drunken police commissioner had rushed Hyberry away from a public dinner, taken him by cab to Clarence Street Police Station, and opened for him a confidential packet of photographs. These were evidence in the murder of a pregnant eighteen-year-old by a gentle thirty-seven-year-old estate agent and father of three. They were properly appalling. The girl's wounds were given a terrible livid tumescence by the photographer's flashlights.

What had the commissioner been trying to do? Display obscenities to stiffen Hyberry's intentions? Rouse in him a lust for the estate agent's death, something to relish during the clinical carry-on of ritual hanging? Force him to morbid joy that the killer would get from *his* hands the hempen reply to the bloody statement which was the girl's body?

He suspected that the commissioner's motives in 1893 had something to do with the Premier's nicety in 1900.

Because Jackie Smolders had been all bewilderment and stupidity at his trial, he had ceased to be murder incarnate. People and the Premier had forgotten that he had chopped up Mrs Newby and kept his head down to the work until ruins alone were left. His hanging had become a mere public duty.

The message for the hangman was that there were drudgery hangings, for which a man could be rewarded, and heartfelt hangings which were somehow less decent. These latter were perhaps too much enjoyed by the hangman and should not be asterisked with a royal honour.

God knows my justice, Hyberry knew, if Premiers and the *Sporting Chronicle* doubt it.

I could resign, he thought. He filled the night with letters of resignation addressed to the Chief Secretary. They were flippant, they were trenchant, they were curt, they were stately, they were explicit, they were an apologia for the craft and virtue of the hangman, they punned, they were as fluffy as de Maupassant, as sonorous and blood-red as Dickens.

But few of them were like him. In fact, none were. He must always be steady and keep his virtue secret, and in that spirit it was hardly worth resigning.

And whoever they then brought in, a new man or a visitor, might fumble and make a mess. It was most important, morally, for the disappointment of all the high and low Knollers, that no one should make a mess of Mr Jimmie Blacksmith.

Mort was a day dead but Jimmie had not heard the shots. Now, in three-quarter light, a mile upstream from the ferry, a patrol of three citizens saw a black man wading into the shallows. With a length of rope beneath his armpits he had cleverly tied a rifle and a hessian bag to his shoulders.

The banks were soft and eroded. The three men dismounted and began to run towards him. He saw them coming and stood for a second defined clearly against the water, tides in balance, tranquil as a set jelly.

This he now broke apart with his sprinting. Suddenly the depth took him; for there is little gradual about the profile of a great flooding river.

Jimmie swam long, pleasurable strokes. Here, in the river, came the peak of his delight at having done the limited rights he could do by Mort and the teacher.

The three pursuers could see him because of the burden he had roped to his shoulder, because—though he made distance with such great panache—he was the only thing that broke up the still of the water.

Now, he told himself, he could make arrangements for

162

meeting death, decide what mode to die in, an exercise he had been unable to think of under Mort's eyes and McCreadie's. He was convinced now that some sort of salvation was in order for Jimmie Blacksmith, and had forgotten the three men on the north bank.

Then a hot hand bore away his left cheek and upper lip. There was more hot blood in his throat than he could swallow. Pain sprang up from cover of mere numbness. For lack of other available protest he swam on, amidst no sound but the considerable one of his arms breaking up the static river.

Nothing else happened. The pain remained in limits, the south bank jolted in his vision, another element in a weird vacuum to which—so he seemed to understand—the men behind him did not belong.

On the south side were no shallows; the river cut a clean bank and he had to pull himself out by the roots of willows. His tongue was intact but swollen, so that it took a long time to probe the injury, for he would not touch it with anything so brutal as hands, and he must keep jolting south from the river and west from the ferry-road.

It seemed that a bullet had entered below the left cheekbone, torn out the teeth of his upper jaw and left through a split in his upper lip. Now that he had left the water the estuary saltiness tormented him.

Yet how spurred he felt by this concrete contact with his hunters. Spurred and freshened. Not towards anything.

It was known now that:

He is south of the river Manning, north of Port Stephens, east of the mountains, and wounded.

The same diabolic energy that set him to his monstrous work last July in Wallah drove him to a remarkable feat in the swimming of the Manning River, though it should be noted that the river was, at that time, at slack tide and favoured his escape. Sydney Morning Herald.

Given that swim, it is a pity that he had a history of female homicide, for it was the act of a hero. Those who minimize it by pointing out that the estuary was at slack water ignore three facts; that the conditions should have favoured a marksman as well as a swimmer; that the river is at this point at least half a mile wide; and that the swimmer accomplished

163

the distance with a rifle and bag of supplies lashed to his shoulders. The Bulletin.

As Dowie and Dud Edwards had felt somehow absolved and justified by being photographed within the ambience of Mort Blacksmith's body, Jimmie felt absolved, justified and even enriched by the swim and the wound, that harsh edge of reality he had kept losing by evading armies.

In this mad intoxication he marched all morning gape-mouthed. About noon he came to a luxuriant place. Two Chinamen and a woman were tending melon-patches, corn, a banana plantation. He used their back door and poured himself a glass of water from the kitchen tap. The workers did not turn, but continued at their wordless harrowing or hoeing. What fine people, the Chinese. Taking their wonderful produce to town, selling it for a song, "Tree-pens, missie"; while the town brats circled their docility singing a mocking song called. "Chingy-Chingy Chinaman".

Now Jimmie felt a gratitude close to tears for them, far off in the clearing, making straight the ways amongst their ripening melons.

He found a saucepan of boiled rice and knocked tiny balls of it, fashioned by his fingers, down his throat.

Last, he found a mirror under a black cloth on a table by the bed in the far corner. Uncovering it, he looked down soberly at the bloating moustache of injury, tilted his head to the left, the better to catch the light.

Blood fell on the mirror and, impishly, to frighten the poor Chinawoman, he left it there.

Higher up the valley, he found shelter under a granite plug, close to a small stream of running water.

The first drying of blood and torn flesh had tightened the wound and he shook his head with infinite slowness on a pillow of blankets; and grew predictably fevered. .

The pain of his mouth became the pain of tooth-excision at his initiation. He dreamt continually of a beautiful mother, a primal Dulcie, greasing her gums and thighs religiously, to aid his cure and birth from the great Lizard. Endlessly she smiled and covered her teeth with unguents.

He was a safe man in his fever, he had done all the things that portended happiness.

164

He passed two nights and a day in the fever, and woke to the numbness of dispossession. What his body craved was honey.

He found a wild nest, a bubo of mud in a tree-fork. At the base of the tree he built a fire and then broke the nest open with a bough.

Inside were the orderly combs which he wedged down his throat in dripping lumps, honey, wax, pupae, God knew what other debris.

He marched and dreamed on foot that he was carrying live coals in his mouth, provider of warmth to someone—Dulcie, old Wilf, Jackie, Gilda, Miss Graf? Doing for that someone a scalding duty.

At last he came to another small school amongst the forests. It was locked and all the children were gone. Could it be as close as that to Christmas? The air was drowsy with pollen and the cicadas improvised the pulse for his great pain.

The residence was locked, but there were no locks on the windows. He got inside, examined the injury in the school-teacher's openly hung mirror. It had become such an indefinite mash of bone and flesh that he felt that it was too risky to probe, even by eye.

He wanted a soft sleep and went through to the teacher's bedroom. Somehow he was at a vanity table, opening the drawers, rubbing the soft feminine fabrics with his hands.

There was a wedding photograph before him. The bride was sharp, small, pretty. The man was square and looked like a policeman. Quick-tempered, to give the schoolkids hell.

Then he was trying a silk scarf around his nose, feeling that the wound needed some sort of compression. A number of letters fell out of the scarf and he bent over to pick them up. All his tender blood ran like loose cargo to his mouth. But he was in that stage of delirium where words torment the brain, when the fevered person reads endlessly from a sort of tortured Bible in his head.

When he opened the letters therefore—they had no envelopes—he read them with crazy dedication.

The first said:

My dear Clarice,
I certainly do not consider it wrong of you, as another's

*wife suffering the ennui of the bush, to write to me. Life is
at the moment too busy for me so that I sometimes feel it
would be a relief to me to have a little ennui. However, I do
understand your need of correspondence to break the loneli-
ness of life in a small settlement. I know that part of the State
well, that the hills come down to the coast, the country is
hard and there is a lot of rain. Never mind, soon it will be
summer and then the forests will be cool, and visited by
breezes that don't blow as far as Macquarie Street or into the
musty chambers of our State parliament.*

*As you could imagine, nobody quite knows which way to
jump now that Federation is on us—very few have made up
their minds definitely whether to remain in State politics or
abandon their State seats to try to be elected to the new Federal
parliament. I have been assured pre-selection for a Federal seat
and a place in the first Cabinet if I am elected. But the chances
of election are hard to calculate, there being no precedents* ...

Jimmie gave up the first one here and opened a second:

My dear Clarice,

*I was delighted to have your last and was very touched by
your predictions of my success in Federal politics. If I thought
that a third of the electorate shared a third of your view I
would have no hesitation at all in resigning my State seat and
launching out. . . .*

*You must tell me if your letters to me and my replies cause
any trouble for you with Clive. I know that he can be a
little morose—justifiably, since the role of country schoolteacher is far below his obvious talents, the gifts he showed
before he gave up university.*

*In the meantime, let me assure you what a delight it is to
hear from you again and that you mustn't think that I'd ever
be too busy. . . .*

*Poor Flo, I'm sad to say, is not well. It is her kidneys. Kid-
neys apparently are mysterious organs. There seems to be
little that any of the renal specialists in Macquarie Street can
do to give her comfort. . . .*

*I am glad that some of the farmers' wives are becoming a
little more neighbourly towards you. They can make life a
living hell. . . .*

166

To Jimmie it was gibberish but he read it slowly and compulsively. The ache in his mouth was numbed now that Clarice's scarf encompassed it.

My dear Clarice,
  Is it possible for a person to fall in love by letter?
  Though that is not the true question: I always loved you and felt tender for you. I delayed asking, and another man asked in my place.
  As for your continual anxiety that I might be too busy at politics to receive letters from a woman whom I have a great affection for, let me tell you that I could not get through my week without your letters.
  Apart from their unlimited value to my heart, they have been like a continuing good omen and under their influence I have finally decided to assault Federal politics in Federation Year.
  Poor Flo is semi-invalided, I am sad to say....

Clarice's correspondent gave some dizzying medical details and said he was sincerely affectionate.

Jimmie opened another:

My beloved Clarice,
  It is ridiculous that I should not be able to see you. I beg of you, leave him. He is a man devoted to failing in life. He is too blunt to succeed. I know his habits are low—you must remember that he was a fellow student of mine—at his rare best and his frequently vile. I have often thought with a chill, and now do so with horror, what monstrous practices he might have tried to force on you.
  I am in a position to instal you in a house in Sydney and would demand nothing of you except your respect and interest....
  Poor Flo, you see, is fatally ill. There is no blinking at that fact. She suffers greatly....
  Two parliamentary leaders stopped me in the corridor yesterday to say that they were looking forward to serving with me in the first Federal parliament....

Names followed. Hard Anglo-Scottish names. The names

of parliamentary sharp practice. Jimmie read it all, and then opened more.

Beloved Clarice,
I have just come from the Hospice for the Dying where poor Flo is in a coma. I desperately regret her going but—please try to understand and forgive me for saying it—I desperately need you. I beg you to come to Sydney. I shall mourn Florence as a true husband should, but at the same time have no doubt as to whom I most wish to entrust my future. If the electorate do not like the idea of a divorce from Clive then they can go hang. My business interests will provide us with a future. . . .

Exhaustion now ran yellow across Jimmie's vision.

My dearest,
I call you my dearest because now you are that. Poor Florence passed on Tuesday. Yesterday she was interred at Waverley cemetery. It was a comforting ceremony and I'm sure that if Florence had only had foreknowledge of it, it would have helped her immensely in her final agonies. The Dean of the Cathedral read the service, her brothers joined two officers of my militia regiment in bearing the coffin. At the graveside was the Premier and all but two members of the State cabinet, as well as the leader of the opposition.
Come to Sydney now, Clarice, when my need of the sight of your face is so sharp. . . .

A last one.

Dear Clarice,
I agree that your recently diagnosed pregnancy puts you in a position where you cannot act freely or come to Sydney. However much it costs me, I applaud your decision to remain with Clive.
At the same time, I have had a professional disappointment. The Federal seat for which I was to have pre-selection has been given to a relation-by-marriage of the State Premier. I have still been assured that my ultimate destiny lies in Federal

politics, but that I must postpone my entry into that arena for a number of years.

It hurts me to suggest this, but perhaps we should cease correspondence for a year or more and let our destinies take on more predictable directions. . . .

I know I can trust you to take discreet action with the letters I have written to you, as I regretfully have with yours to me.

Be assured of my undying respect.

Yours,

E

Lunatic duty done, he went to sleep in the schoolteacher's bed. About mid-afternoon he woke to noise. From a window he saw two men on horses riding about the schoolyard. One dismounted and came towards the school residence.

Jimmie made for the back door. He seemed to be pushing a massive pain before him, but was able to unbolt the door and hobble westward into the forest.

Some minutes later, Dowie was looking down at the schoolteacher's bed. There was a wide cloud of blood on the pillow.

"The filthy bastard," he said, as if Jimmie had somehow defiled the schoolteacher's marriage.

15

———

I N a lucid moment at night he crossed a bridge to a low misty town called Kaluah. There had been rain, and frogs drummed in the mudflats.

On the town's first hill stood arched windows with lights behind them. He heard the rat-tat-tat of nuns praying aloud. A person could fit any words to the clacking chant and, in Jimmie's state, did.

God have mercy on poor Mort Blacksmith, young voices called.

Taught to kill women by his bastard brother Jimmie, older and huskier ones responded.

Outflanking the chapel, he came to a lighted kitchen in the side of a two-storey house. Tall jugs of milk were in the ice-chest. Like a Spaniard drinking wine he poured some from a distance down his throat. Beef stood on a large salver and he dropped shreds of it into his mouth, willing his swallow to give them transit.

Then into a hallway. Bare buffed boards stretched beneath two kerosene candelabra, unlit. It was an ample hallway. The church built on a European scale, even in Kaluah.

All down the walls, saints' faces softened with the joy of Christ-God. They could be seen by strong light from a half-open parlour door. Well down the hall he could see beyond the door to a someone who was, beyond question, dying.

170

It was a small middle-aged nun in a high-backed up-holstered chair. She seemed severe, but that could have been the disease. It had thinned her body within her robes, withered her face so that the top of her throat could be seen beyond the gamp.

She had been excused chapel.

Now he had to fight with the crazed concept that to give himself up to her would be a surrender of special merit, that it would emphasize to everyone how much he wished all were restored again. Jackie Smolders to his tribe, Mrs Newby to Mr Newby, the Newby girls to their hearty country finery, Miss Graf to her squatter's son, Mrs Healy to Mr Healy, the baby to Mrs Healy's breast, Toban to his inheritance. His grave regret would be signified by the gravity of this dying confessor.

However, he might as an alternative simply go to bed. The further arm of the hallway ended where someone had gone to the trouble to paint in gilt on a cedar door: *Guest room*.

Inside there was carpet on the floor, such fine carpet that it would have done to sleep on. There was a fine white-quilted three-quarter bed that had had so little recent use that it had settled itself to the slump of its mattress.

Little else he could see by the light from the hall—a cabinet, a washstand. Drawn blinds. Four pictures. Saints persisted in their especial visions in three, and the fourth was a photo-graph of a fat clergyman who would have fitted into the basin-shaped bed.

Jimmie Blacksmith closed the door gently against the dying nun and mauled the white quilt down. Then he went straight to sleep.

When he woke up in that high benign bed it was daylight beyond the blinds. In the distance Dulcie Blacksmith was speaking in an Irish voice, "But that'd require a special arrangement. I'd expect to receive a letter from His Lord-ship's secretary first. Really, some of these clergy! . . ."

"Come on, Dulcie," he said. "None of that flash talk."

When a woman's shoes were heard nearing the warm March embankment where he drowsed his hand cast about for bull-roarer, his head filled up with its thrumming and the

171

woman, in terror of the Lizard, turned and pattered away.

It was night again and he was clear-headed and thirsty. But he waited till he could hear nothing but, deep down in the dark, the chant of nuns.

He let himself out. From the dark end of the hall he sighted the sick nun, tonight lying blank-faced on a sofa. Another nun, whose back was to him, occasionally wiped her face with a damp cloth. Jimmie coveted the moisture in the cloth but had no compulsion to surrender. Finding the kitchen, he ate and drank in his gape-mouthed way.

His mouth had, in fact, been cruelly asymmetrical in form, so that though there was a corner of teeth left to him to use, he could not chew with them unless his bottom teeth on the right side bit at the swollen mess of his upper jaw. It tantalized his mind, the way his mouth had been sculptured in the womb to turn against him in his final crisis.

He had sliced mutton to take back to bed with him, apricot preserve, biscuit, a jug of water. Confident as a drunk, he travelled with them back down the hall.

The ministering nun was reading to the moribund one:

. . . just as St Bernard of Clairvaux chose a swampy marsh as his monastic foundation, setting for his monks the twin test of clarifying the waters of a morass at the same time as they clarified the morass which is the soul of man in its natural state. The waters of contemplation sing with three sylvan notes: they are clear through their unity, their clarity is the clarity of diamond for there is no atom in them averse to the scalding unity of the divine light that shall illumine them. . . .

Of course, Jimmie told himself, the waters by which you grow to be man are clear. The perch and the crayfish are set in them as in diamond. They admit the light. Not only that, they break it into long crystalline spangles and hurl it back in your young eyes.

Then he saw that his eyes had fixed themselves on the shine of the light on burnished board, that he was tottery; that the apricot preserve was slipping out from the hold of his left elbow.

He adjusted his arms and went back to his tall ecclesiastical bed.

He slept and his wound pained on. As any rebirth wound could be expected to.

When he was conscious and remembered how he had got the wound, he fell into a worse delirium.

Often it was the lurid corner where Mrs Healy had died between the dresser and linen cupboard. Those he loved were there considering with shoppers' interest the bloody remnants.

And Mort—trust Mort!—was the first of them who got the idea of painting himself with tints from the rotten traces of Jimmie's old hatreds; painted his cheeks and chin with dipped index finger and looked at the effect in a glaring mirror on the left of Jimmie's vision and seemed happy with it.

So intently, no indecent gaiety, they all began, competing with patterns against each other. They would not be told or warned off. Their purposeful limbs faded from his hold.

Then Farrell rattled about. All at once, Jimmie was in a hospital. He had never been to one before yet recognized it by its solemnity.

His churchman's bed lay beside that of a naked white boy with neatly sown hare-lip. The boy was to be married today but was fatally sad. He could not be persuaded to put on his wedding suit.

And so on. Jimmie slept in hell.

One day the sun struck at him, quick as a blow. Something had gone wrong. It had flown beneath the dark rafters. His legs were hot under bed-clothes. His jaw was milder. The teeth they had ripped from him had begun to itch.

Then a cunning door in the forest opened and into the heart of tribal secrets stepped Dulcie Blacksmith.

He threw his arms about. It was well established that they would be damned by seeing each other.

But bloody Dulcie would not be stopped. There was a sternness he had not been used to in her face.

She said, "My poor man, you've done so many evils and suffered so much."

From the *Bulletin*:

There is great irony in the fact that the notorious homicide-cum gynocide-cum-infanticide should have been found in a dignitary's bed in a country convent. Sister Cecilia entered the guest room of Kaluah Ursuline Convent to prepare it for the visit of His Lordship Bishop Thomas Grogan. She found a swollen-jawed aborigine, surrounded by corroded pieces of food, in a delirium in the bishop's bed. She ran in terror from the room—not for a moment thinking that she was eligible for £2,500 in reward money. It seems that a citizen's arrest was then made by Reverend Mother Evangelist.

Jimmie Blacksmith is now recovering in Kaluah lock-up of a wound contracted two weeks ago when a stray bullet from one of his pursuers damaged his jaw.

Meanwhile the bishop's sheets are being thoroughly laundered. It seems that while the flower of the manhood of east and west were pursuing him, Jimmie had spent four days at least in the convent's guest room and foraged for food while the nuns were in chapel singing their office.

The *Bulletin* was the work of safe city-dwellers, who could afford to be flippant.

Dowie Stead and Dud Edmonds were one day late to Kaluah. It made Dowie feel hollow and ridiculous that Jimmie Blacksmith had snared himself in the guest room of a convent.

They remained in Kaluah two or three days but it became obvious that Jimmie would not quickly recover.

"He's still an outlaw," said Dud. "Yer got a right t' go into the lock-up and shoot him."

Dud was right, legally speaking. But Dowie did not have the nervous energy, after the long dismal ride, to act with such Mediterranean force.

To complete a pattern he felt to have been imposed on him, he went south and joined the army. His father wrote to him complaining that because of his enlistment they would have to hire a manager for the property. Could he visit stock and station agents in Sydney and find someone honest and capable and preferably unmarried? Jessie would perhaps keep such a man happy.

Dowie failed to complete the ideal and necrophiliac Romantic pattern: he did not die at a Boer's hands. By the time he reached the Southern Transvaal it was difficult to find a Boer to pay you the compliment of a bullet.

174

A letter (published) to the Editor, the *Bulletin*:

Dear Sir,

It appears from a report in your edition of January 15th, that the jailhouse parsons are already at work on Jimmie Blacksmith. It all reflects on the ridiculousness of hanging such a murderer. As a man of primitive mind, and in the hot-house atmosphere of the condemned cell, he will be easily persuaded of the prospect of heaven for the repentent sinner and will therefore die easily at a nominated time by a humane method.

Why then hang him? It is no punishment. If a murderer must be punished, if punishment is the motive behind the hanging, should not the public executioner be permitted to enter Jimmie Blacksmith's cell at an unpredictable hour and cut him to pieces with an axe?

Either do this to him, or leave him in prison long enough for boredom and doubt to enter his bones, so that he will die in doubt at some unpredictable time. After all, this is the "punishment" we all suffer, a heavier one than hanging.

I say too, keep the parsons away from him. They will not awaken him to his guilt but rather drown it in false comforts.

Yours sincerely,
Tom Dancer,
Secretary
Union of Wharf Labourers

A letter (unpublished) to the Editor, the *Methodist Church Times*:

Dear Sir,

I believe that I carry some responsibility for the recent sad history of atrocities committed by the half-caste aborigine, Jimmie Blacksmith. It was I who, lacking any definite instructions on how to proceed in the management of a mission station, encouraged particular ambitions in Jimmie Blacksmith —the ambition to work and complete work, the ambition of owning property, the ambition of marrying a white woman.

As inexcusable as Blacksmith's crimes are, there was almost certainly some white provocation of the young half-caste, especially in the matter of his marriage to a white girl.

So that one wonders if society is yet ready to accept the ambitious aborigine. And the question then arises, what should we, as pastors, do in regard to our black or brindled flocks? Should we raise our own kind of hopes and ambitions in them, ambitions of industry and honourable labour, of increase and ownership of property, connecting these hopes and ambitions to the message of Christ? I certainly thought so once, but wonder now.

Should we, as an alternative, attempt some amalgam of Christianity and the native spirit? Is such an amalgam possible?

If we cannot readily answer these questions (I make the point because I cannot myself and must rely on more enlightened colleagues) we must examine carefully our role in native mission camps and even ask ourselves what we are doing there at all.

I humbly request all your readers, sir, to pray for the repentance of this murderer who once lived under my roof; assuring them that due to his imprisonment, he has come to a lively sense of horror for his crimes against Christian men and women.

> *Yours etc.*
> *Rev. H. J. Neville*
> *Muswellbrook, N.S.W.*

Mr Neville was permitted to visit Jimmie, who was shocked to see him. Mr Neville had, in Jimmie's mind, always connoted a black gloss of clerical certainty.

Now he looked like a man who had surrendered. The black silk of his clerical stock was worn at the collar bone to show the stained buckram beneath. The notebook in which he took down the names of people to whom Jimmie wanted him to write letters of goodbye and repentance was full of fluff, and the pencil so blunt that he had to work lumps of wood away from the lead with his fingernails.

Jimmie got a terrible feeling that here too was one of his victims and was glad that distance and duty kept Mr Neville from visiting him more than twice. The young parson from whom Jimmie was contracting his jailhouse fervor was natty and unblessed with doubt.

Jimmie had not liked Mr Neville's stammer of laughter when he said, "What I git sorry about is I never had no good woman to love an' respect, like you and Mrs Neville."

Of course the trade unionist was right. Jimmie Blacksmith underwent a fundamentalist conversion in jail. In the early days of his recovery he had been beaten up by policemen—in Kaluah, on the ship to Sydney. More blood in his throat to go with the sea sickness.

But in Darlinghurst, that kingly jail near the Hospice for the Dying, he was treated well though coldly, and a chaplain was kind and opened his heart to Christ.

The sweetness of it carried him through a swift trial in December. In the dock, he told how innocent Jackie and Mort and Gilda were.

Then Australia became a fact.

It was unsuitable, too indicative of what had been suppressed in the country's making, to hang two black men in the Federation's early days.

Press cartoonists sketched the nascent motherland. She was young, with shoulders like a boy and a firm mouth. In one hand she held perhaps a tome with a title such as "British Civilization", in the other a blank parchment entitled "The Fresh New Page of Democracy".

She rather resembled Miss Graf.

Easter came and filled centre-ring at the Showground with hearty rams and wide-snouted bulls and stallions from Lismore, Moree, Cobar, Coonabarabran, Kiandra, Jerilderie and all the nation's strange-entitled towns.

People laughed in their state of grace, the old crimes done, all convict chains a rusted fable in the brazen Arcady and under the roar of buskers in temperate April 1901.

And the other viciousness, the rape of primitives?—it was done and past report.

Scratch a Labor politician and even some of the others and you find twentieth-century daring. Votes for women. Pensions for the old and for the widow. Industrial courts benevolent to trade unionists. Had anyone in London, Paris, Vienna,

Washington even hinted at such eventualities? You could bet your bottom dollar they hadn't.

So the candy-floss was eaten in sunny April, the spring of the southern world. Men from Quirindi and Deniliquin rode mad bulls. Men from the cedar forests behind Nowra, Kempsey and Murwillumbah, dressed in athletic vests and white pants, raced each other at log-felling, and the summered biceps of a mettlesome gaucho-people flew in the high sun on the day of Christ's crucifixion.

They knew they were good. They knew they were strong. They knew they were free and had a fury for equality. The *Bulletin*, after all its irony, kept saying so.

It was happy Easter and open another bottle as the wild men pitched over the necks of crazy bulls from Wyalong.

You couldn't hang blacks on such an occasion.

And all the time, Jackie Smolders, his murders now nine months gone, was sequestered from all hints of his tribe and tribal landscape. The walls of Dubbo jail shut out all moieties and totems, and the *tjuringa* could lie broken in its holy cleft. Jackie Smolders, wrapped away in the utmost privacy of quarried stone and mortar, had become concerned with his immortal soul, as his nephew had.

In May Mr Hyberry went to Dubbo and hanged old Jackie. It was a quick and easy hanging.

The next day Jimmie saw an eye he was not used to, peering full, blinking rarely, at the Judas window. A new warder? Jimmie wondered. A politician? Jimmie, on the second last day of life, had the prisoner's thirst for novelty and eye for small changes.

Mr Hyberry was away three days in all, and his fine boys could cope with the customers.